MY SILVER LINING

MY SILVER LINING

A Novel

Rachael Ruble

Illustrated by: Chris Nicolosi

authorHOUSE®

AuthorHouse™
1663 Liberty Drive
Bloomington, IN 47403
www.authorhouse.com
Phone: 1-800-839-8640

Published by AuthorHouse   09/20/2012

ISBN: 978-1-4772-7326-5 (sc)
ISBN: 978-1-4772-7325-8 (e)

Library of Congress Control Number: 2012917761

Dedication

I dedicate this book to my loving husband who surely thought I was wasting my time. He helped me get through this and is my number one fan and editor. He is also a domestic God, taking care of the house and our children when I suddenly had a brain storm and just had to write it down. For you Bry. I love you.
It is also to my children who I know can do anything they set their minds to, just like their mom did.

Acknowledgements

I would like all my friends and family who stood behind me during the process of writing, proof-reading, editing, and finally publishing my first book to know that I appreciate you. I love you all.

My friend Mike is a techy computer genius when I thought all was completely lost. He saved the day. A few times.

Chris and Alyssa I thank you for the art work and putting up with my craziness.

Chapter 1

She would never, ever, not in a million years, pass up the chance to own a piece of something to call her own, Ruby told herself as she left her mortgage company in Bluffton. She was behind a few months worth of payments and the man in charge of the account had the audacity to ask her if she had some land to put her shop, "Chicks Trucks" on. He had to have thought about that question before he asked it she thought. Could he really be that stupid? If she had money for land why in the hell would she put up with his aggravating company with their agitating rules? Ruby was in her truck driving down the main highway when her phone rang, she answered, "You got Ruby, "it was her assistant Brad.

"Hey boss, you need to get back here ASAP some guy is here asking why he's waiting for his jeep when it has been here for three days already."

"Tell the guy I'll be right there."

"Will do."

Ruby ended the call and drove as quickly as she could manage without breaking any speeding laws. God knows she didn't need anything else to pay for. When she got to her shop she noticed a rather large man standing near Brad with his arms crossed over his chest. She got out of her truck and walked over to find the man talking about how hard it was to work on a jeep, because of the small opening. She interrupted just as she would with anyone else and said, "They aren't hard to work on unless you don't know what you are doing."

The man and Brad turned around, Brad was smiling, but the man looked surprised to hear a woman's voice.

"And just who might you be, young lady."

"Wow, I haven't been called a young lady in quiet some time. I'm the one responsible for all of the work that is being done on your jeep."

"Oh. Really. I thought there was a Brad working here. Someone that might be more up to the task that it requires."

"It's not that big of a task. I can handle it."

"No, it's not that I don't think you could handle it, I just thought there was a guy here and not female mechanics."

Ruby could tell he was trying to make his statement seem like a nice one but she knew he wanted to say, what is a weak woman going to do to my truck that a strong capable man can't do? Ruby kept her fake smile intact and through clenched teeth she said, "I'm sorry you came to that assumption. The name of the shop is Chicks Trucks not Chicks and Trucks. I am the only certified mechanic here, you talked to Brad on the phone and your jeep will be ready tomorrow, the parts store sent over the wrong spark plugs and that is where the delay came from. So, if you want to yell at someone give me a minute and I'll have Brad find their number for you."

"Oh no that's okay, I heard that there was a woman working here, but I assumed that she was the secretary."

"Well, no sir, you heard wrong, and when I finish with your truck tomorrow I will give you the name, number, and directions for an all male shop, okay. I'll see you tomorrow."

She did an about face, military style and walked away from that sexist pig swearing to herself that if she hadn't she would have hit him with a monkey wrench; and that wouldn't get the bills paid or do her shop any good.

"Thank you! Five o'clock, finally! Brad clock out, I'm ready to get out of here. I have a date."

"I didn't know you started dating again?"

"I didn't, I stopped looking for dating material. There's no one decent out there anymore who wants a smart woman that knows how to work with her hands. My date is with my bathtub and a beer."

"Alright then you have fun with that, see you tomorrow."

"Yep."

The ride home was the same as always but she was slightly more annoyed because of her conversation with her customer this afternoon. Ruby got into her apartment and wanted to call her best friend so bad, but it was late and she was tired. She went into her kitchen and got her beer out of the fridge and headed straight for the bathroom. She watched her body in the mirror as she stripped off her low rise jeans and white grease-stained wife beater that she wore to work. She considered this outfit as her uniform since she had so many of them. Simplicity was definitely her thing, plus jeans and t-shirts were an easy thing to come by and why on earth would she force herself to wear those coveralls that the mechanics wore in the old days. It was anybody's guess. She loosened her hair from the tight bun it was in and her curly, chocolate-caramel colored hair fell loosely around her heart shaped face and shoulders. She didn't get out to much, so she had always been really fair skinned.

She used to joke that the sun shone right around her because she was so skinny. She stripped out of her leopard bra and her large handful of breasts fell free, then she stepped into her tub. She had no use for underwear so she refused to deal with them unless absolutely necessary, which was when she had a date. Which lately just seemed to be a never needed piece of clothing. While laying against the inside of the tub wall she decided she would call her best friend Cindy in the morning, she knew she would be up because she had a horse ranch on her property, and that meant getting up early to feed everyone.

After thinking about Cindy and her husband Scott and their three children, Ruby's mind started to wander and she was thinking about her other friend Shannon. Shannon got married two years ago to Josh and they have one son. Ruby wanted a family to call her own so bad but when she was younger she had her fair share of problems, who didn't? But she felt like she had to grow up fast. Her stepfather had been a huge part of her life. He taught her how to drive a truck, how to change the ball bearings on a boat trailer axel, and they even built a large playhouse together for her younger sisters. So even though she was only twenty-one, she felt very accomplished, she had her shop and she only had to pay one kid; who thank god worked for minimum wage.

Ruby knew she had it rough, but she didn't let it get to her, and she didn't want sympathy from anyone. She went through two divorces with her mom, and went to visit her dad a couple of states away for two weeks out of the year until she was sixteen and got a job. Her dad was a military man and when she and her sisters would go to visit they would spend a lot of the time with him at the beach. Those were very good memories. She knew she couldn't think like this. She was going to start crying soon and once the flood gates opened there was no closing them until the pipes were completely empty.

Truth was she missed her family. She had moved away after graduating high school. She told her family she wanted some life experience, and for her that meant making her own decisions. She moved about two hours away from her family and found a cute little apartment. She took no time moving in and even met a couple of her neighbors. Since she was the shy type she didn't feel comfortable going about looking for men. She just couldn't quite see herself as the woman on the prowl.

Ruby was climbing out of the tub when she thought of her mom and how she told her that if she needed anything, even if it was just to talk, to call her. It didn't matter to her mother what time of day it was. Ruby knew she would always answer the phone. As Ruby was slipping on her night clothes she shook her head. Her lonely feeling had left just as fast as it had come and now there was no need to call her mother. Ruby slipped under her covers and thought back to the days of high school when she knew everyone and everyone knew her. That did it. She fell fast asleep, the remaining thoughts in her head turning into her dreams.

Ruby woke up early the next morning, made her coffee then jumped in the shower. She remembered she wanted to call Cindy and decided she would make it a quick call because she really wanted to finish the spark-plug job in the Jeep before the owner got to the shop. She hated it when men in particular watched her work, it made her nervous. She thought about the last man that she let watch her work and then said, "asshole," he only wanted to get into her pants and she was not like that when it came to men, she actually was hoping to wait for the right man, hopefully that day would come before she turned thirty. Actually a bunch of her high school boyfriends tried that with her, and she quickly found out the way to apparently make a man "happy," and she wasn't willing to go down that road.

Ruby suffered some hell when she was growing up. It wasn't all picket fences and apple pie. When a guy made an attempt to have sex with her she thought she was in trouble. He had been a nice guy at first-maybe that was because he already knew what he wanted-and then as she repeatedly turned him down he became nasty and forced himself on her. She had survived his attack because he was a little shrivel of a man. She survived and at that moment she knew exactly what men wanted and knew that nothing could stop them when they had what they wanted in their sights. As it turned out she was still hopeful that there was a good man out there in the world somewhere, just waiting for her.

Ruby actually did find one nice guy a year ago his name was Bryan or Byron but he was with a customer of hers and she figured that meant that they were together, so she didn't look into it or try anything. He had helped her out of a sticky situation when she first opened her shop. He didn't know it was her shop, or if he figured it out, he never said anything to her.

Some crazy guy came driving up into her shops parking lot yelling at her and telling her that she totally screwed up his truck and it almost blew up with him in it. Byron walked up to the guy and told him to calm down or he would call the cops. The guy yelled a few choice words about women working on trucks in Ruby's direction and then Byron pushed him so hard that he fell down to the ground, and Byron told him he better go on and never come back here again. When the guy left, Byron turned to Ruby and told her that if the guy ever came back here he wanted her to call him. She promised and thanked him, and she meant it. She wasn't sure if she would have been able to diffuse the situation, so she was very happy and grateful that he did. Byron or Bryan and her customer left in her customer's car and Ruby never saw him again.

*   *   *

Ruby ran into her closet with her phone on her shoulder. She was telling Cindy that they needed another girls day soon or she was going to crack. As she was talking she pulled on her light blue holey jeans, black bra, and a wife beater, then reached for her socks and yanked them on. She and Cindy were etching details in stone when she got into her kitchen. Ruby grabbed her chrome thermos and filled it with her black coffee and set it on the table, she told her friend she loved her and thanked her for listening to her rant and rave. She hung up then reached down to pull on her brown steel-toe boots.

She grabbed her bag and her coffee and headed out the door. After her eight chimes from the elevator, the doors opened to the parking lot and she walked to her trusty truck with keys in hand. She jumped into the truck that she rebuilt and headed out of her parking lot toward her job. She drove a 1985 Ford Ranger, it was painted navy blue with thin hot pink stripes down the sides, she put super swamper mud tires on it and added a hot pink lift kit to it last year, complete with hot pink springs. She had finished detailing her truck earlier this year. She added a chrome grill, fog lights, and on top of her truck what she called, look out lights. She loved being in her big truck, she couldn't imagine having to ride in one of those tiny little sports cars. She always had the fear of being run over. There was no way she was taking a chance on her fear coming true.

When she pulled into her parking spot she saw Brad getting out of his moms van and heading her way.

"What are you going to say to that guy when he gets here?"

"Nothing, I am going to tell him his truck is ready and then you are going to give him the name, number, and address of some other shop. Where men work."

Ruby sipped her coffee and went to find the spark plugs, she was totally calm. When she had all eight of the spark plugs in her grips she headed for the Jeep. She was lucky she had small hands otherwise this job would be a real pain in the butt. The guy was late according to Ruby's clock. When he finally arrived, he said he was giving her time to finish the job. Brad busted his chops by saying," Dude, she had your Jeep done in like, thirty minutes." The man looked shocked but as promised Ruby handed him the piece of paper with her competition on it and then added, "If they get a spark plug job done with-in an hour, with bare hands, I will be pleasantly surprised."

Then she turned and walked away toward her office. She scooped up today's paper on the way to see what could possibly be going on tonight. The news around Bluffton was always slow and nothing really happened here like the way it did in big cities. The news was boring, the comics were funny, the advice sucked, and there were no single people searching for their soul mates. She flipped it to the last page of the paper and saw the movie schedule, the romantic comedy, "Love is funny to me" would be playing. Now suddenly she had plans with herself and she was going to look nice damn it, even if it was just for herself.

She and Brad left work at exactly five o'clock again today. She had already told him where she was going, although she wasn't sure why. Brad was sixteen and she was twenty-one. She didn't consider him old enough to understand her problems. Brad's mom came and picked him up and then Ruby left. She always made sure he had a ride before she left. She wouldn't be able to stand worrying over whether he got home or not. Brad was a good kid that got in trouble vandalizing her shop and he was working for her to pay her back for the damages. She decided to be nice and let him keep half of what he made because he was saving up for a car. He was a good kid underneath it all, and he was one hell of a hard worker. She believed it was peer pressure that made him do it.

Chapter 2

The ride to her apartment was about ten minutes long and then it was another fifteen minutes to the movies. She pulled up into her spot in the parking garage and headed inside to the elevator and pushed the button for the eighth floor. When the elevator doors opened on her floor a few people were fighting to get in while she wanted out. Crazy people, she thought as she unlocked her door and went in. She locked it behind her as always, and then headed for her closet. She figured since the movie would be a romantic comedy maybe she should dress a little softer and nicer than usual. More feminine. She found a black skirt that was mid thigh and a pink tank top. She didn't think she owned a skirt or anything pink, Cindy must have snuck it in there the last time she was here. She slid on her black stilettos—she needed all the height she could get—and headed back out the door.

She got back down to the garage and climbed into her truck and she took off. She didn't mind going out, even if it was just with herself. She cared what other people thought about her, but she knew how to mask it so it seemed like she didn't care and that became something she almost believed herself. That it didn't bother her, that is. Although, if they stared too long she would understand the look. It would seem like they were reading her innermost thoughts, she was alone, and as of right now there was nothing that she could do about it. She pulled up in the theater parking lot and climbed down out of her truck, and she saw a few people looking her way when she headed to the double doors.

Ruby told the woman behind the counter what she wanted to see and the woman handed her a ticket. Next was the snack counter, Ruby had to have a Pepsi and she decided on a medium, she didn't want to float out of here tonight. She had refused to eat sweets or popcorn from the time she hit her teenage years, and since there was nothing else at the snack counter, she simply walked away. When she got into the theater she realized it was a little slow tonight, everyone must be here to see the big action blockbuster, she thought. She was never big on action unless there was lots of blood and guts involved.

The movie started right on time, and she didn't need to go to the bathroom until about half way through it. She stood slowly and grabbed her drink and her bag and made her way to the door. She noticed that she wasn't the only one who needed a break, and quickly went through the door. She was heading to the bathroom and wouldn't you know it, a line. She looked over and the men had a short line too, and then she saw him.

Byron Miller. The man that helped her out of the sticky situation at her shop.

He left his place in his line, walked right up to her and said, "Hey, I remember you. You're Ruby, right?"

"Yes, and you're Byron? You helped me out once before."

"Yeah, I can't believe you actually remember me. Are you here with someone?" Byron asked her.

"No, I have a "date with myself" tonight.

"Wow, tough to beat that one. How do you qualify for a date like that?"

"Well you have to be totally unattached and I am all the time. How about you? Are you here by yourself too?"

"Yeah, all alone. I seem to find people who think I'm funny, but not in a good way. Hey, are you seeing "Love is funny to me, too?"

"Yeah why?"

"Well how about when you finish up in the ladies room we can go finish the movie together, no one should sit through an hour and a half of romance by themselves. What do you say?"

"That sounds great. I'll be right back."

"I'll be waiting right here."

Byron wouldn't have believed what just happened if he hadn't seen and heard it with his own two eyes and ears. He remembered Ruby very well. He remembered how it felt to shove that guy when he had the nerve to call her a bitch. No one was going to talk to a lady like that with him standing around. He proved his point very well. The man left and she never called him about the guy coming back. He had hoped she would call just so they could get together or go out. But alas, he thought he scared her with his brute tactics. He remembered her being violently upset at what the man called her. He wanted to comfort her but he wanted to hurt the guy more. If she had let him he would have hugged her or something. She didn't know him and he thought better of his idea. She was so pretty, he remembered. She was greased up like she had been working on an engine or something. All he knew was he wanted her then and seeing her now got him happy again. In his heart.

Just as he promised her, he was waiting on her when she came out of the bathroom. She walked slowly so she could take in his appearance. He was wearing light blue jeans and a white wife beater underneath a blue plaid button up shirt, he had his hands in his pockets and he was smiling at her. It gave her a very warm, fuzzy feeling.

They walked back into the theater and sat through the rest of the movie. The ending was a real tear jerker, but she refused to ever let anyone see her cry, so she did a lot to hold it back. By the end of the movie she was wanting to talk to Byron some more, since they didn't get a chance to during the movie. She was sincerely surprised when he asked her what else she was doing tonight. She replied with nothing, and he said, "You want to go and get a cup of coffee and catch up?"

"Absolutely." She really didn't have to think about her answer.

Ruby was thrilled with seeing Byron again after all this time. He had helped her and she never forgot a kindness. Especially one from an olive toned man that now seemed to be slightly interested in her. Her. They went and had their coffee and talked for hours on end closing the shop down. When they walked outside Byron kissed her lightly on the cheek, it was a small sweet gesture that moved mountains in her eyes. He had asked her out again and they were going bowling the next weekend.

*   *   *

She was happy now more than ever because she and Byron were seeing each other. She couldn't remember ever having this much fun with any of her previous boyfriends. She loved his company, but what she couldn't get over was that old adage "All the good men are dead, gay, or married". He wasn't just a good guy he was a great guy and he was hot. And he wasn't gay or married. Just drop dead gorgeous. Jackpot!

When she first saw him that night at the theater, it took everything in her not to pinch herself and tell herself to wake up. She thought it was a cruel nightmare at first. His hair was curled down around his eyes, but it was short everywhere else and so dark it looked black, he had a jaw line that you instantly wanted to kiss, even though he had a trimmed moustache and goatee, olive tone tanned skin, and a very chiseled physique that was easy to see, especially through his white wife beater he had on. He could easily be described as every woman's wet dream. Although, the first thing she noticed about him was that his eyes were the exact same color as hers. A perfect sapphire blue, she had never seen anyone with her color eyes before. Against his tanned skin it made his eyes even more appealing. She thought about his eyes and her eyes and their intensity, and how they matched, then thought, well, it must be a sign.

She wanted to see the rest of him, to see if there were any more signs to be found. They had been very good since they started seeing each other, he hadn't asked her about anything intimate, and they would give each other little pecks for kisses every now and then.

They were supposed to meet outside of the coffee house beside her job, and she decided at that point that she didn't want to tell him that she owned the shop and what she did for a living, she would wait to see if he would draw his own conclusions and then see how this was going to play out. She didn't want to spook him or jump the gun. She didn't want him to think she was too rough around the edges. No matter how much she actually was.

Byron got to the coffee shop about ten minutes after Ruby and ordered his coffee black with sugar, she didn't realize how tall he was until just now, he towered the woman at the counter. When he sat down at the table with her she asked, "How tall are you?"

"Six foot five. Why? Does that make me too tall for you?"

"No, I was just curious."

"How tall are you, and what do you weigh? I feel like I might have to reach out and grab hold of you when a strong wind blows." He said with a lop-sided grin.

"I am five foot six and I weigh one hundred pounds exactly. And before you ask, no I do not, nor did I ever have an eating disorder. I have always been small, but I am also very athletic and I took gymnastics, so I am very flexible."

He arched an eyebrow at Ruby and with a grin said, "Really now? We may have to explore that flex-ability thing a bit further later on."

"If you think that it's necessary, I could give you a performance."

"What kind of performance?"

"Well how about one day we can go to the beach and I can show you a cartwheel, a round off, and maybe a back bend."

"That back bend sounds interesting. That would be fun for other "activities".

"Well, I hate to tell you Byron, but I don't know how to do those kinds of things, aside from what I have read and what my friends have told me. I have never had sex before."

"What? Why?"

"You would be the first guy that got to get that close to me. Every guy that I ever dated has been a complete asshole, so I would dump them before they got the chance to try and make a move on me."

"How is that possible? I can't believe what you're telling me. You are a virgin?"

"Yeah, so? Do you think that makes me strange or something? You watched The 40 Year Old Virgin didn't you. At least I'm not that old. I'm proud of myself that I didn't give in and give it up to some random loser."

"No, Ruby. I think you are anything but strange. I am actually amazed that you told me. I don't think I know of any virgins. Plus, you are so attractive that I just find that; well, very hard to believe." Ruby blushed at his comment, she liked it that he called her attractive, but it would be a long cold day in hell before she actually believed it.

"Shut up, I am not beautiful. I'm a grease monkey and I'm a tomboy and I always have been. Nobody has ever called me that, and I don't think it should start now."

"You my dear are in serious denial. Do you see the way men look at you? They are not looking at a grease monkey mechanic; they are looking at a hot female working under their hood thinking what every other man in America is thinking about."

"Oh, yeah and what's that?"

"That they wouldn't mind looking under your hood. It's not everyday you get a sexy, voluptuous woman in a wife beater, covered in grease stains working on a big truck. It really is a mans ultimate fantasy."

They sat there arguing about Ruby's sexiness for the better part of the morning. Byron kept throwing sexual comments in Ruby's direction but she didn't care. Since it was Saturday and she didn't have to go to work she asked him if he wanted to go to the beach and of course he did. He wanted to do whatever would let him see her, dressed or half-naked it really didn't matter.

"Ruby, I just have to run by my place and grab a change of clothes, do you want me to meet you back here?"

"Yeah, I can be back here in like twenty five minutes how about you?"

"Thirty maybe, if I push my truck."

"Perfect see you soon."

"Bye."

Time passed quickly, it was no time before they were back at the coffee shop and he offered to drive her to the beach. Apparently he hadn't seen her truck because he didn't say anything about it. When they arrived at the beach it took a few minutes to locate the perfect spot, when Ruby found it they laid out their towels. Byron quickly yanked off his t-shirt to show off his totally chiseled body. Ruby wanted to reach out and touch him, but she fought the urge. Ruby started unzipping her denim cutoffs and Byron felt as if he was getting hard just watching her. He quickly lay down on his stomach to hide his large display of sexual wanting. He lifted his head up to see that Ruby had already removed her shorts and was about to pull her shirt up over her bikini top, he noticed she had her belly button pierced and it had just a plain sapphire gem in the rod. It was very sexy. He was leaned up just enough so that he could see her easing herself down on all fours to lie on her flat stomach, and that was when he spied a small tattoo just above the front of her bikini bottoms. Because it was so small he bet that it probably went a little farther than her bottoms were supposed to. So much of it was covered up that he couldn't make out what it was. She was wearing a black triangle top that she was spilling out of, not that he was complaining. The bottoms were Brazilian cut so her butt cheeks were visible on both sides and damn, she was wearing her bikini right, he thought.

When she got laid out and comfortable she leaned over to Byron and said, "Would you mind rubbing some of this on my back, I burn easily."

"Sure, babe, if you show me your tattoo."

Ruby looked at him like she didn't know what he was talking about then reluctantly she rolled onto her back a little and eased her bottoms down so her tattoo was visible. She had a red dashed line leading down about two inches then a black X. It hit him like a kick in the groin.

"You have a treasure map leading to your umm, "treasure".

"It was a dare, when I was eighteen. And no, I don't regret it, but I wish it had been something else."

"I think it's sexy, you should show it off more." Byron said, grinning from ear to ear.

"Byron, shut up."

Ruby rolled back over to hide her tattoo, and so Byron could rub her down with the tanning lotion. When her face was down he sat up slowly, realizing that he was still erect and still trying to hide it from her. He didn't want to do anything that would spook her, or do anything that she didn't want to do, and he was going to have to be patient with her. He grabbed the bottle of sun tan lotion from her hand and squirted it on her back; she surprised him when she reached back and pulled on the string in the middle of her back to untie it and said, "I hate tan lines." He grabbed the untied strings and laid them to the side, and that's when he saw her breasts pressed down and out underneath her. Byron realized he was staring at her and had to collect himself before Ruby realized he was staring at her. He slowly worked the lotion into her skin and could feel what felt like tingly sparks of electricity between them. Whatever it was, he liked it. He couldn't stop at her back. He squirted some of the lotion onto his hands and then rubbed them over the backs of her lower legs, then worked his way up slowly to her thighs, and then he rubbed at her butt cheeks that were hanging out. When she felt him rubbing at her bottom she had moved her head so she could look at his face.

She could see his droopy, half closed eyes and knew exactly what he was thinking.

"Byron, we can't do that here."

"Do what?"

"Whatever is making you feel that way."

"What way?"

"You're horny, I may be a virgin, but I'm not a moron. I can see the signs. Plus, I told you I didn't know if I was ready, yet."

"Well then I guess I need to make it clear, you are the only person on this beach that makes me feel this way. That bikini wouldn't look good on anyone but you. I'm not trying to pressure you Ruby, I just can't help myself. I like how it feels touching you."

"Wow, Byron, I like that you like touching me, and I think you reached your limit of sweet comments to give me for this week. How many women have you been with, if you don't mind my asking?"

Byron stopped rubbing on Ruby and lay down beside her and stared into her eyes.

"Two. One was a girl that I met about four years ago and we were together for two years, the other decided it wasn't worth working out after we had sex. I never really thought about her after that, but that was about seven months ago."

"Good enough, I mean you haven't been waiting as long as I have but at least you didn't get your last romp last week."

After they had baked in the sun for hours Ruby reached back and tied up her bikini then got up, she decided to keep her promise and show Byron some of the more flexible things she could do. So while still in her bikini she stretched and then she started by doing cartwheels, and she was surprised when Byron copied her. But, he couldn't do the round-off or the back bend. When she leaned back and planted her hands in the sand for the back-bend, Byron walked all around her and eyed her entire body then decided to go under the bridge. He crawled under her and lay on his back. When Ruby's arms got tired she dropped right on his chest. He wrapped his arms around her and hugged her close. They stayed right there, in that spot on that beach laughing at each other and making jokes until the sun set over the water. It was very romantic.

Chapter 3

Two weeks after Ruby and Byron went to the beach, Ruby found herself wanting to spend more time with Byron. She didn't think she would ever want to spend any time around any man. What was he doing to her to make her feel this way? Whatever it was, she liked it and didn't want it to end. They were going out again tonight. Byron wanted to take her out to dinner at the new Italian Restaurant in town, called, Mama's Cucina. Which translated to English means, Mama's Kitchen.

When they got inside the restaurant Byron gave the hostess his name. The hostess immediately grabbed two menus and somehow managed to seat them in front of about ten other couples in line and Ruby started to wonder if he had said something to the hostess. They got a nice table near a window, and with candle light. It was so nice, she liked this. She had never been anywhere fancy before and she hoped this whole romance thing would rub off on her. He seemed to be a romantic kind of guy and she had never met a man like him before. He liked sunsets, candlelight, and holding hands. He knew how to talk to her, and he knew all about her family, and now she wanted to know about him.

"Do you have any family around here?"

"My mother and father died three years ago, I have no siblings and all my cousins and aunts and uncles live out of state. When my mom passed, I took over her store, and that is my main source of income. I already told you about my past lovers. Yeah, that's about it."

"Wow, that was . . . . brief."

"Well, you know about my past and now I want to know more about your past."

She didn't want to tell him the story, but figured that if they were going to have a working relationship it was best if he knew. She had never told anyone about what happened, not even her family. Should she really trust him with her deepest darkest secret? It was a sore spot for her that brought on nightmares when she thought about it too much. But she figured if she told him she would feel better about it, too. Maybe venting it out for once could help her out after all.

"I will tell you whatever you want to know as long as I can go back to my place and tell you. For privacy reasons."

He agreed, and added, "I can't wait to see your place."

The waitress came out and took their orders and poured them each a glass of wine and Byron wondered what she would tell him when they got back to her place. He stared into her eyes hoping to find the answer within her, but all he saw were her sapphire blue eyes twinkling back at him. Their dinner finally came and it was delicious. Byron ordered the Chicken Marsala with the fettuccini, for the both of them, and told Ruby it was the best thing on the menu. If Byron hadn't asked her to come here with him she never would have come alone, so she would have missed out, big time. When they finished dinner Byron ordered Tiramisu for dessert and kept control over the spoon and plate and fed her bites of the dessert. She felt special tonight and she was ready to come clean about her past, with Byron.

Byron called the waitress over and told her he was ready for the check. She started digging around in her apron and then pulled out a kitchen check and told Byron that the owner took care of it already. He gave his thanks and asked her to tell the owner thank you for him and he would see her later. Ruby was curious again, but didn't say anything, yet. They walked out of the restaurant hand in hand until they got to his truck. Byron walked Ruby to the passenger door and opened it for her.

"Thank you, sir."

"Your welcome my dear."

"Byron, how did we get seated so quickly ahead of everyone else, and why didn't we have to pay?"

"Ruby, I have connections in this town, and what do you mean, why didn't *we* have to pay, there is no way in hell you are going out with me and paying for your own meal, I don't believe in all that "going Dutch" crap. Only a cheap man that isn't interested would do that to a lady that he really liked."

Ruby looked at him with a sweet smile and said, "You really think I'm a lady, and you really like me?"

"I know you're a lady and yeah I really like you. I remember how you looked at the beach, no one but a lady could look like that, and if I didn't really like you then I wouldn't have looked at you like that and wanted you as badly as I do."

Ruby sucked her teeth at Byron then rolled her eyes at him and said, "You are such a strange man, yet so sweet and honest I like that about you."

Byron started the truck and Ruby directed him to her apartment complex and showed him where to park. The other spot that belonged to her apartment was right beside her truck. Now she would get to see his reaction to the real Ruby. He parked his truck next to hers and looked at her with wide eyes and said," Wow, I wonder who drives that truck, and how tall they must be!"

She was happy he didn't say, "How tall he is." Now she felt like she had a fighting chance. She looked at him and said, "Byron, that's my truck, I drive it everywhere."

"Really? Do you use a step ladder to get into it?"

"No, I told you and I showed you, I took gymnastics and I'm very flexible. I simply stretch my leg up to the bottom of the door and climb in."

"Seriously? That's really your truck? Babe, you are so short."

"Yeah. So. Tall people drive small cars, so I am a small person that drives a big truck. Big deal."

Byron went around to Ruby's side and opened her door and helped her out. Then Ruby led Byron through the lobby and into the elevator and pressed her button for the eighth floor. She started digging around in her bag and pulled out her keys. When the elevator doors opened she took off to her apartment with Byron right behind her. When they got inside she asked him if he wanted a drink and he asked, "Do you have any Dr. Pepper, it's my weakness?"

"You are in luck, my best friend Cindy loves Dr. Pepper, and as it so happens she left a few here."

She was coming back from the kitchen when he sat down on the couch. She hesitated for a second, but then thought what the hell I'll have to tell him at some point. So she started telling him about what happened back when she was sixteen.

"When I was sixteen I started dating this guy. Well I thought we were dating, we never actually went anywhere. He said he liked me a lot then after about a month of seeing me he tried to put his hands on me. I told him that I was not interested in sex. He laughed at me and said that anyone that came into contact with him was ready for sex, she just didn't know it yet."

Ruby noticed that Byron was visibly upset and she could see him tightening his fists.

"He pressured me a few more times and I kept telling him no. It was cold one afternoon when he stopped by my parent's house. They were at work and I was all alone. He knocked and I let him in. Now I regret that decision. He walked in the house and pushed the door closed behind him. He approached me slowly and asked who was home. When I said no one was home a sick grin crossed his face and he launched himself at me. He knocked us both to the floor. He slapped me across my right cheek, and while he was sitting on top of me he started ripping my clothes off."

Byron was grinding his teeth together, and shaking his head while he took shallow breaths.

"He freed himself from his pants . . . . and that's when I woke up crying. He was scared, it's like he didn't know what he had done. He looked down at my naked body beneath him, he looked visibly sick and even when he tried to penetrate me, he looked like he was going to throw up. I realized what was happening with him and tried to scratch and bite him but I couldn't get a grip on him. After a few minutes of trying to get inside of me he gave up and left without a backward glance. He never approached me again after that day.

Then she told him, "There is no need to worry about it now. I know who he is and he will forever be a asshole in my eyes, he was a guy that didn't know what he was doing, so even though he tried to take my innocence, he couldn't, he just wasn't strong enough."

"I can't believe you went through that. You didn't tell anyone?"

"You are the first to hear about it. I'm sorry to lay this at your feet. But honestly, it is nice to talk about it for once."

She noticed he was slowly calming down because his knuckles were a natural skin tone again and not liquid-paper white so she moved on to her teenage years, with all the boyfriends that tried to talk her into sex, but they got absolutely nowhere.

"I knew I was damn lucky to escape my past with my virginity intact so I always treated it like it was something I didn't want to give up unless I was happy giving it up. When many of my ex's would try to push and persuade me into it, they realized how head strong I was, and if I didn't want to do anything, then it wasn't going to happen, end of story."

"I'm sorry you had a crappy childhood. No one should have to go through that alone."

"It's okay, really, I'm not mad anymore. I have had so many years to stew over it that it doesn't really even bother me anymore. I only get nervous and agitated when I see that asshole. He came to my shop one time when I first opened and when he saw me standing in the bay glaring at him with a pry bar in hand he backed up got into his piece of crap car and never came back."

"Tell you what Ruby, if you ever see him again and I'm still around, by the way I hope you want me to be, I will break his hands and beat the holy hell out of him for you."

"Thank you for that, but it's not necessary. I won't go as far as to saying I have forgiven him, it's more like I forgot most of what happened. Like I blocked it out. It's a good defense mechanism that I seem to have adapted."

"What do you mean?"

"Well, one of my more recent ex's asked me about something that happened over a year ago, and I simply could not remember. He said we argued over it for two days straight. But I have no idea what it was."

"Damn, I hope I never cause you to forget things on purpose."

"I don't think you could be mean enough to make me forget things even if you tried."

As soon as Ruby stopped talking about the ex's they both started yawning.

"I don't want you driving home tonight, you are too tired and it's so late. Plus the deer in this area are everywhere. Just crash here tonight, okay. You can even sleep in my bed if you want and I'll take the couch since it's so short."

"Sure, I'll stay. But I am not going to let you take the couch. Now go to bed woman."

"Alright, if you're sure. Thank you for staying and thank you for tonight. I really had a great time."

She leaned down and gave him a peck on the cheek and told him goodnight. He returned her goodnight, and added a sleep well. Ruby left Byron in the living room and headed for her room, when she was inside the sanctity of her bedroom she changed into what she normally wore to bed, boxers and a tank-top, no bra and no panties. She preferred comfort when she slept, but she refused to sleep totally naked. What if a fire broke out, there would be a fireman getting a show. Ruby threw her overstuffed pillows on the floor and she climbed into her bed and under the covers, and she was asleep in minutes.

Byron couldn't believe his ears. She was raped without the rape actually happening. She had been scared to death and the asshole had the audacity to hit her. How could anyone slap a face that looked at sweet as hers did? He couldn't wrap his head around it. It was wrong on so many levels. The fact that she hadn't told anyone said volumes to him. She didn't like to feel vulnerable and that was what this made her feel. She hid this nasty secret for six years from her parents, her family, and her friends. She felt ashamed and he didn't like that one bit. She was too beautiful to feel ashamed. She was his from now on, he decided. He could treat her like no other man before him and she would never want to leave. He didn't want to see her leave. He kicked off his shoes and took off his belt and his button down shirt. He lay back on the couch and placed the crook of his elbow over his eyes. Falling asleep was going to take concentration.

"NO, NO, NO, STOP, PLEASE STOP! NOOOO . . ."

Byron jumped to his feet and ran into Ruby's room flinging the doors open so hard that they hit the walls behind them. He thought someone was breaking in. He saw Ruby kicking and screaming in her sheets, but she appeared to still be sleeping and apparently having a nightmare. He ran to her side and shook her awake, and she jumped as if he had just scared her, and not the other way around. As soon as Ruby saw him she started crying and Byron knew he wouldn't be getting any more sleep tonight.

Without asking her opinion, he climbed into her bed while she cried. She grabbed his naked waist and hugged him close to her while she let her tears fall onto his bared chest. She never wanted anyone to see her cry, but that damn dream came back again. She hated reliving the nightmare of her molester, and Byron didn't like the fact that some asshole had the ability to make her have nightmares about what was done to her. He laid there in her bed combing his fingers through her hair and whispering sweet words of safety in her ears as he kissed her temples and her cheeks until she passed out again. He felt as though he was doing something wonderful because she started to smile in her sleep.

Chapter 4

After waking up in Byron's arms, totally dressed, Ruby felt relieved. She was so sure that he would have tried to put a move of some kind on her, but he didn't. Her slight movements woke him up and the first thing out of his mouth as he was staring at her was, "Wow, how do you do that?"

"Do what?" Then she yawned and stretched.

"Look beautiful with your sleepy blue eyes and matted curly hair; you know you still managed to make my heart skip a beat or two?" She didn't know what to say no one had ever seen her in the morning besides her parents and sisters, and they certainly never said that to her before.

Ruby blushed and said, "Byron you make me feel beautiful."

She leaned down and kissed him lightly, then backed away. She didn't want to scare him away with her morning breath. He smiled at her, he wanted more of that, morning breath be damned, but he would never take what she didn't want to offer him. He wasn't the monster from her past, and because of that guy, Byron was going to make sure to be extra careful with her. She didn't need to have a break-down.

"You hungry?" Ruby asked Byron.

"Sure, but coffee is fine you know."

"I was hoping you would say that. I have to go to the store soon."

Ruby was standing in front of the fridge, bent over slightly and looking in. Her fridge was a little on the empty side. Byron was watching her as she was slightly moving her hips. Apparently dancing to a tune in her head. He couldn't take it. Byron had to force himself to go get dressed. He wanted to sit there and stare at Ruby all day, but that wouldn't help him out in the long run and he knew it. Then he remembered what was going on tonight.

"Ruby I want to take you out tonight. Have you ever watched a pool tournament?"

"No, why?"

"Well, I am part of a league here in town and the tournament is tonight at the bar where we usually practice. Would you like to go with me and be my good luck charm?"

"If you think you need good luck then maybe I could beat you a little."

"Great, then I'll be back at seven tonight and we'll go to the bar."

He leaned in and placed a quick little peck on her cheek then he turned around and was out the door heading to his truck.

*   *   *

This had been the longest day in history according to Ruby. All she wanted to do was go out with Byron, and her kitchen clock was ticking by so slowly. She decided to paint her nails and then fix her hair at about five o'clock. She had to give herself something to do before she started cleaning her house, again. She went to her closet and chose her outfit and the shoes.

Later on while getting ready for her date she realized he was something totally different from any guy she had ever met. She had a rougher unpolished side and she was going to learn how to get a softer side if it took months, just so she looked a little more feminine to him. He had seen her get really dirty and he had even heard her burp really loud at her house, but he never saw her do anything really lady like. She didn't even know if she liked that phrase, lady like. Yeah she was a woman, but she grew up like one of the guys. That was just how girls are when they are raised in the south.

She was ready when she heard Byron knocking on the door. She checked herself in the bathroom mirror once more before going to let him in. He was early, but she liked a man who could keep a good track of time.

He greeted her with a kiss and a whistle and said, "Wow, wait till the competition takes a look at you. They're gonna miss-cue every time."

She looked down at herself and said, "Too much? Should I go and change?"

"No way, you look hot. I don't think the guys will even believe you're with me."

He looked down, seeing for the first time that she looked like she was going to a bar. She was wearing a black halter top that was low cut so her cleavage was pushed up at the top, and a pair of low cut black leather pants that looked painted on and he could see her belly button ring and the first few red dashes of her treasure map tattoo, followed by a pair of black stiletto boots that he loved for her to wear.

He loved them as much as she did because when she wore them he didn't have to lean down so far when he wanted to kiss her. She surprised him when she reached up and grabbed the collar of his blue polo shirt and pulled him down and kissed him hard on the lips breaking his concentration. Then she pulled away just as fast.

"Let's go babe, don't you need to practice or warm up or do whatever it is that you do. I don't want you losing your tournament because of me."

"Yeah, sorry. I got a little . . . . distracted, let's get out of here."

With that they were gone, heading for the parking garage, and his truck.

When they got to the bar he figured since it was slow he would go ahead and practice a little. Ruby was all too eager to help him practice. He came up behind Ruby to help her hold her cue stick and show her how to use it. She didn't fight him, she liked that he was this close to her. After she beat him twice out of four times he looked at her and said, "You never said you knew how to play."

"Well you never asked and I figured I could hustle you a little. So we'll call it a draw, because I don't want to make you think you are going to lose tonight. Plus, I like the way you showed me how to shoot."

"Thank you for that, really. Now are you ready for wings and beer?"

"Absolutely."

They found two seats at the bar and ordered the hottest wings and the coldest beer. After nibbling through half the wings, people started crowding them at the bar. She guessed that meant it was time for the tournament to start, she spun her bar stool toward her man leaned over and kissed him hard enough to force her tongue into his mouth, something that nearly knocked him off his barstool. He stayed right there, put his hands at work holding the back of her neck and kept that kiss going until one of his buddies tapped him on the shoulder to tell him it was time to start. He didn't want to stop this kiss, but he felt her pull away so he did stop and she said, "Good luck out there, I'll be cheering you on from the sidelines."

"That was for good luck? Wow, what do I get if I win?"

"I don't know yet," she said with a little smirk and a twinkle in her eye. That smirk plus the outfit she was wearing was going to make it hard—or rather him hard—to concentrate on what was going on during the game. Oh, she was going to torture him with the way she looked tonight. She had her hair down and those soft curls framed her face, the black halter top she was wearing was almost see-through. He wondered if she planned this, then thought, that's okay I can resist temptation for as long as she can. I hope.

When the tournament was finally over Byron came and found her on their stools and said, "You really are a good luck charm. I managed to get second place."

She was very happy for him, and glad that she helped in some small insignificant way. She liked giving herself to him for that kiss and not freaking out when she liked how he tasted and how he felt against her. She then realized that she must really like him, maybe even love him. Maybe it was time for her to let go of that one thing that she had been holding on to for so long, and let someone love her, that would treat her right.

She was on her way to the bathroom when some drunk jerk stood up, slapped her on the ass and said, *"Hey there! Damn, you got a nice ass. Why don't we get out of here, just you and me?"* Before she could think of something to say to this asshole, her reflexes kicked in and she reached back and then lunged a fist forward with every ounce of power she had, and punched him right in his nose. He immediately let her go and grabbed his nose. Byron appeared out of nowhere at got behind the jerk and had his arm twisted around and pulled up behind his back while he was bleeding profusely. Byron informed the jerk that if he ever wanted to use a cue stick with two hands again he had better apologize to his girlfriend or it would get really ugly in here. It was the single nicest thing anyone had ever done for her. The man finally apologized and left rather quickly holding his shirt on his nose. Smart man.

It was so cool how masculine Byron was, he took control from her and showed that drunk loser who was boss, but he was more impressed with her reaction to what that jerk did to her.

"How . . . Did . . . You . . . Do . . . That?"

"Do what?"

"Punch that guy like that. Ruby, you know you broke his nose, right?"

"Yeah, that's what was supposed to happen. Now he'll probably think twice before he tries to slap someone else's ass again."

Byron grabbed her wrist-not wanting to hurt her hand if it was broken-and said, "Does it hurt?"

"It's nothing really. It's not broken; it only hurt when I made contact with his nose. "She was smiling when said that and Byron took notice.

He pulled her hand to his mouth and kissed each knuckle gently while he grinned at her and she said, "All better." Then it hit her like a ton of bricks, he was her silver lining from those black clouds from her past. His love could outshine those clouds completely. She knew she had to have him, all of him, and all to herself, tonight.

"Ruby are you ready to go home or do you want to stay here a little while longer?"

"No, we can go back to my place and hang out for a while. If you want to." she said while her eyes were becoming narrower by the second.

He realized she was looking at him with that same face as earlier when she kissed him. That devilish grin and those twinkling eyes were going to get her into trouble he thought to himself.

"If you're sure you want to, then I would be happy to go to your place."

Ruby got right up to his ear and said, "Good, let's go. Because I am sure that I want you. Tonight!"

"First I need to run by the drug store and get some condoms."

"I don't want "anything" to come between us. Besides, I'm covered."

God, the way she said "anything" really had him trembling all over. She was even talking sexy and Byron wasn't sure she knew it.

"Me either."

Byron said it in a low husky voice that caused Ruby to grin at him.

She wanted him so badly that she could hardly see straight. She wanted to see his body again, she could hardly remember that day at the beach. Then she thought, I have no idea what to do with him when I get him home. So that means he gets to be my teacher, too. They arrived at her apartment complex in relatively good time and then they were almost sprinting to the elevators. When the elevator doors opened and revealed her floor she already had her keys out and in the lock by the time Byron got to the door. She let him in first and followed him locking the door behind her.

He leaned down and kissed her gently then pulled away at just the right moment and asked," Ruby are you sure you want to do this? There is no pressure. I can wait."

"I'm sure I want you, because you are the very best thing that has happened to me in a very long time and I'm not about to let you get away, again."

The statement caught his full attention. He looked at her with confusion setting in all around him.

"Wait, what do you mean, again?"

"Well, about a year ago when you helped me out at the shop, you were with one of my customers and I thought you were really cute. I also assumed that you were together."

"Well, in that case I have some making up to do for the past then, don't I?"

Before she could form a sentence he was kissing her in a way that made her skin feel like it would burst into flames. Then he pulled away again and said, "You're sure."

He didn't need a response to understand what she wanted. She wrapped her arms up and around his neck then kissed him softly and when his mouth parted slightly she was ahead of him. She slipped her tongue into his mouth and their tongues danced against one another. She reached her hands higher and grabbed two fists full of hair and held on tight as he pulled her body to his, until they looked like they could have been connected, there was no room between them. She freed one hand from his hair and ran it down his chest and she could feel every one of his muscles tighten, and she could also feel his thick erection rubbing up against her heat. He kissed her more deeply and she gave him everything she had.

She had never had a kiss like this in all of her dating ventures. He was so gentle yet strong, and hot for her. Her. He placed his hands on her plump bottom and picked her up while still kissing her. She wrapped her legs around his waist and he made his way to her bedroom. He had noticed the large, plush, king size bed with its antique inspired wrought iron work and four posts at each corner the other night when he held her, and never thought much about how it would feel beneath him when he was naked, but now he couldn't wait to find out. Slowly, he lowered Ruby to the bed and began kissing his way from her soft sensuous mouth to her jaw line planting little kisses in the hollows underneath her ears then down her neck, and he surprised her when he bit her over her jugular, she made a little squeal of delight because she liked it and then her whole body broke out in goose bumps, and he noticed.

As soon as he saw the goose bumps he starting rubbing her arms, trying to make them go away. As he went back to kissing her neck, he could clearly see two swollen peaks beneath her halter top and he was amazed that she was this easy to turn on. He started rubbing her nipples through her halter top and then worked his way to her neck where he untied it and then pulled it over her head and flung it across the room. Now all that was in the way was a black lace bra.

She wasn't totally unaware of what was going on because while still sitting she realized that his erection was now sticking straight up, which was quite a task in those tight blue jeans he was wearing. She wanted to reach out and touch him, but she didn't know if she should yet, she didn't want him to think she was pushy or rushing into this.

Byron beat her to the punch, he asked her in a low deep growl by her ear if he could take the rest of her clothes off and all she could manage to get out was a long whispered, "Yes." He pushed her back on the bed and grabbed her leg into his hands and removed her boot and sock and then went to the other leg and did the same thing again. In that low growl of a voice he was using now, he said, "I like the way you look when you wear these. They make you tall enough to kiss me back."

His thought of seeing her completely naked was going to cause him blindness, his eyes kept rolling in the back of his head as he planted little kisses along her ankles. He pulled her to her feet and started unfastening her super tight leather pants then helped her to lie down on the bed so he could simply pull them off. He grabbed a handful of leather at each ankle and tugged at the material until they were at her thighs. He leaned up and saw she was wearing a black thong that matched her bra. Black see-through lace.

"Damn baby, that's sexy!"

He leaned over her and started kissing all the exposed skin around her thong. He kissed her up both sides of her panty line and then moved higher to kiss her hipbones and then back down both angles of her of her feminine divide. At this point she was losing her mind. He noticed her eyes had rolled back into her head and he knew he was giving her great pleasure. Byron liked the fact that he could do this to her, for her. He also realized that he liked the taste of her bare skin. She tasted like vanilla in the summer time. He leaned down again and tugged her pants off the rest of the way and began kissing his way up her leg until he met her panties then kissed her down the other leg.

He looked up at her and by this time she was looking back at him, he reached his hands to her hips and tugged off her panties in one swift motion. He let out another low groan when he saw her landing strip. He couldn't look past her curvy hips, he wanted to taste her and feel her warmth. He eased her thighs apart and could see the wetness of wanting that she felt for him; there was no hiding this sign of love.

"Ruby, I need to see how long you can last," he said, while eyeing her package. "So just relax a second, and let me, umm, test you out."

He lowered his head to her southern region and began lapping and kissing at her velvety folds, she felt like heaven. He had only just begun when she started whispering, "Byron, oh god, yes!" He realized she was climaxing.

"Ruby, that was really quick. We'll have to see if we can't slow you down a little bit."

He picked himself up from between her thighs and reached behind her to unhook the bra that was keeping her hostage. The bra fell away and her breasts were free. He immediately leaned down and kissed the swell of her breasts and then sucked one nipple into his mouth, teasing her, then he gently bit at her and it sent goose bumps throughout her body, yet again. This time he could see the goose bumps went to every inch of her body. He was looking at her and she could feel the heat of his gaze, but she didn't feel the need to shy away from him. She liked the way it felt to be all sprawled out for his hungry eyes. She really liked the way he was looking at her. She felt wanted, sexy, and needed for once.

Since he had stopped doing his sexy little things to her she figured it must be her turn to return the favor, so she got up and asked him to take his shirt off since he was so much taller than she was. He took his shirt off and had it on the floor before she could blink. Slowly she traced the outlines of his torso and his muscular biceps with her fingertips. He tightened his pec's and she moved over with her tracing. She seemed determined to trace over every muscular outline of his gorgeous chiseled body.

"Your muscles are so big and sexy. You are so strong. I love the way you hold me in your arms."

She made her way down to his legs and removed his shoes then his socks. Then she stood up so she could tackle his jeans. Ruby was having trouble getting the top button undone because Byron was so excited, so he helped her out and then he started to unzip his pants when she grabbed his hand in both of hers and said, "No, I want to do this part."

He stood there motionless like a statue of a hard Greek God while she unzipped his jeans and then gasped as all of his manhood jumped out in front of her. He realized at that moment that he had forgotten to tell her how he was big . . . all over. Literally. She paused then looked at him with her devilish grin and that twinkle in her eye;

she knew what she was supposed to do. She stripped his jeans down the rest of the way and made her way back up to his boxer briefs, which were clearly not doing their job anyway since he was able to escape them. She had them off of him in record time.

She got down on her knees between his legs and made her way to his happy place, then she pushed him back onto the bed and crawled her way up between his thighs. He lay back with his arms crossed behind his head; he didn't want to interfere with whatever technique she was going to come up with. She grabbed his shaft and noticed that her finger tips were not even touching. He was huge. She quickly relaxed her mind; she didn't want him thinking she was scared. She was ready. She leaned down intending to take all of him into her mouth or at least try, but it just wasn't possible, so she kissed and sucked on his member while listening to him moan and make hissing noises under his breath.

He couldn't take it anymore. He sat up and pulled her onto his lap and noticed that her wet spot was pressed right up against his thigh. He liked their bodies being naked together, and he liked knowing that she wanted his body just as badly as he wanted hers. She was wet for him and he couldn't wait any longer, if he did he was sure he would explode on her, and somehow that just didn't seem right for her first time. He had to act fast. He pushed her onto the bed on her back and kissed her mound one more time for the moment. He pulled himself up and looked in her eyes with lusty need in his hungry eyes.

"Ruby, if I hurt you, please tell me. Don't play it off as nothing. Being this big isn't always a blessing and I don't want you to get hurt."

"Byron, I know there will be some degree of pain, but if you don't make love to me right now, it will hurt more. I need to feel you inside of me."

Byron moved directly over the top of her and was holding himself up as he kissed her passionately. He placed his shaft right at the entrance of her love canal, then looked at her and said, "Ruby look at me, I want to watch your eyes. She made a small cry of pain when he entered her and then she went very still. He noticed tears rolling down her cheeks, while she was still looking at him and he became scared.

"Ruby are you okay? Babe, please, talk to me."

"Yes, Byron, please don't stop" she whispered, so without pulling out he nudged into her lightly, just a few more times and then he came. He stayed there buried inside her for a few more minutes while he kissed her and caressed her body, and he told her how great she was. When he pulled out he noticed she was trembling and crying so he held her until she calmed down.

"Ruby, really, are you okay? Please don't lie on my account, you won't hurt my feelings."

"Byron, that was very different from anything I have ever done. Yeah, it hurt a little bit, but I want to do it again, with you. Only you."

"I would love to do that again, as much as you want even, just not tonight. Okay? I really, don't want to hurt you. If I do I don't think I'll ever be able to forgive myself."

"Byron, I want you, and I would forgive you."

Chapter 5

Byron jumped up and said, "I'll be right back." He ran into her bathroom and turned on the warm water in the Jacuzzi tub and set the pulsating water to a low speed. He was determined to make this night special for her no matter what he had to do. He found some bubble bath and candles and when everything was set up it smelled wonderful, like a field of calming lavender in her bathroom. Quickly he walked back into her bedroom and scooped her up, he had her cradled right up against his tight muscled chest that she liked so much, he kissed her sweet and light as he carried her to the tub and gently sat her down inside of it. He looked at her and said," Don't move, I'll be right back." She didn't even speak, she only nodded her head to acknowledge him.

He made his way down the hall to the linen closet and found spare sheets. He carried them back to the bedroom and tossed them to the side while he removed the bloody sheets then replaced them with the clean ones. He carried the bloody sheets to the bathroom with him and tossed them in the hamper. He looked at Ruby in the tub, she had her eyes closed, and he thought, this woman really is my version of heaven. The way she was leaning in the tub and had all the bubbles around her body made her look like an angel floating on a puffy white cloud. He would never be able to resist her.

He got into the tub and sat behind her, and she leaned her body back against him. They both could feel the electricity flowing between them. He turned her slightly and began kissing her again, then stopped and said, "Ruby whatever is going on between us, I don't want it to stop. Ruby I think I'm falling in love with you." She looked at him and said, "You really think so. Because I'm falling in love with you, too. You are the only man I have ever felt this comfortable around, I have never felt comfortable telling anyone about my past and I think that counts for something. I love you, Byron."

"I love you too, Ruby."

Byron knew how he felt about Ruby, but he didn't know she felt the same way. It was weird for him to hear someone other than family say, I love you to him. Yet, here he was with this beautiful woman and she said those magical words first. He sat in the tub with her until they were both wrinkly and pruned. When they got out of the tub and dried off she walked slowly to her closet and handed him a pair of her larger boxers. He looked at her questionably and she said, "Relax, they're mine. I sleep in boxers and wife beaters."

"I wasn't worried about who's they were. I just can't believe how relaxed your style is. Don't women usually wear night gowns or lacy things to bed?"

"Byron, I wouldn't know. I have never felt the need to dress up for a man before you came along."

He started to reach for his clothes and she said, "No, please, stay tonight, I want your arms around me when I wake up in the morning."

"Ruby, which side of the bed is yours?"

"I sleep on the right. I like being far away from the door when I sleep."

"Why is that?"

"Well, I always have bad dreams and one of them consists of a man coming into my room while I'm asleep and . . . Well, I'm sure you can figure out the rest."

"That's messed up. Don't worry. Tonight, I'll be protecting you from who-ever-it-is."

"That's why I love you, Byron. You are so protective of me. No one has ever been like that with me before and I like it. I like feeling safe."

"I love you so much that nothing would make me happier than to lay beside you while you sleep. Don't worry, I'll keep watch."

With that being said they got into bed and were spooning under the covers. This was new to her, but she liked it and she didn't want it to stop. She felt so at peace with him beside her, that she fell asleep within minutes of him wrapping his arms around her. She slept soundly all through the night, with no nightmares, and she was pretty sure she didn't snore last night.

The next morning Byron woke up before Ruby and kissed her sweetly on the cheek because the night they just had was so sensuous he wanted to do it again, everyday, with this woman. She really did look like an angel, sleeping there with her soft curls around her face and she was murmuring in her sleep, she kept saying, "hmm" and "umm." He got out of bed and went straight to the kitchen and started the coffee. He looked in her fridge and found the eggs and decided making breakfast would be a nice touch. He scrambled the eggs and poured Ruby a cup of coffee and then carried it into her room and set it on her bed side table.

The smell of the eggs instantly woke her up. She smiled and said, "Honey, you shouldn't have." He shot her back a smile and said, "Please." He asked her what she had planned for the day, and she said she was going to work from home on her laptop, even though it wasn't necessary. So he suggested they go out to his place, he had been wanting to show her where he lived but her place was closer to town, so they just came here. He was proud of his place; it was left to him by his parents when they died. He knew that the house was in the family's name and it should have gone to him when they died, but he was expected to put it up for sale and use the money to pay off their final expenses. Instead he was shown an insurance policy that he knew nothing about and it was more than enough to cover the costs of burials and their final expenses.

After breakfast they had a bit of mid morning fun, since neither one of them had bothered to get dressed yet. He said, "It seems like a waste to just cover up your body without exploring all those curves again." She held on a little bit longer this time and it didn't hurt quite as bad as last night. For that she was grateful. After their morning romp he went into her closet and helped her pick out her clothes, then he recycled his clothes. He chose her black stiletto boots, a pair of low cut, holey blue jeans, and a wife beater, she usually wore her wife beaters to work and sleep but she was nice enough to go along with it. He had gone through her lingerie drawer and had chosen a white G-string with a matching white bra and then he asked her if she would wear her hair up.

She then realized that he was turning her into this sexy woman that he had been apparently imagining. She felt like her usual self, but a little bit sexier with Byron watching her. They headed out of her apartment and into the parking garage to get his truck. It was high up there but not quite as high as hers. He held the door for her and watched her climb in before he closed the door and headed to his side, got in, and started up the engine.

On the way to his house this morning he was surprised by her. He thought that she would have needed help to get into his truck with heels, but no assistance was required, and she had done it before. He liked that part about her, but he was still surprised. They were maybe ten miles from his house when he ran over a nail and his tire popped and went flat. He started cussing blue streaks and swearing at everything that moved. He told Ruby, "I am going to set fire to this piece of shit then roll it off a cliff."

"You can't do that now, it only has three good tires."

He laughed then said, "The truck has a spare, hang on while I call Triple A. I think they fix flats."

She gave him a perplexed look and said, "Why would you call them when you have a mechanic on call all the time?"

"I don't know. I guess I don't want you to get dirty."

"Well, that's tough. I'm bound to get dirty, no matter what I'm doing. The work I had to do online today was order spare parts. So have no fear your mechanic is here, no Triple A wing nut needed."

He looked at her dumbfounded and said, "I never thought that I would get to see you in action on my truck in a million years. Even though you are *my* mechanic."

"I know. Today's your lucky day, baby."

She got out of the truck and looked under the back seat for the hidden panel so she could find the jack and the lug wrench. When she located them she yelled out, "SCORE." He was still shocked beyond all reason. She got the spare tire out from underneath the truck bed, rolled it to the flat tire then placed the jack in the right spot under the frame. Before she lifted the truck she loosened the lug nuts, then she jacked the truck up and took the lug nuts off the rest of the way, switched out the tires, and replaced the lug nuts, tightened them up and then let the truck down. She rolled the flat tire to the truck bed and asked Byron if he would help her put it in the back of his truck.

"I can't lift it, it's too heavy. I can patch it up at my shop when ever you want to bring it by."

Byron lifted the tire over his head and tossed it into the truck bed as if it weighed ten pounds. After gathering everything up and putting everything away, they were in the truck and on their way again. She kept feeling him watching her, but she didn't look over, all she could do was smile. She wondered what was going through his mind right now, what could he possibly be thinking about?

Byron was wondering how this little woman could do a job that was made for a man like him. He was grateful that they were not still stuck on the side of the road, but still kind of in shock. He wished he could have been able to change that tire, or knew the basics of how to even change a tire, instead Ruby had done it and gotten dirty in the process. Although looking at her now with black smudges of dirt on her arms and wife-beater and one under her eye from where she wiped at sweat with her forearm, he thought she was the sexiest mechanic he had ever seen. He wanted her again, right now.

Ruby looked over at Byron and noticed that his pants had become a pitched tent, and quickly asked, "What are you thinking about?"

His response was jaw dropping. He pulled over to the side of the road and got right next to her ear and whispered, "I want to put myself inside of you, right now." She gave that devilish smile again, and he knew what was going to happen next. She reached over and unzipped his jeans and bent over him and took him into her mouth and started kissing and sucking.

"If you keep that up you'll be getting covered, and I don't have anything in here to clean up with."

She picked her head up and slid over to her side of the truck and started taking off her jeans and thong, she was going to enjoy this, she thought. She climbed onto his lap in the driver's seat and eased herself down onto his swollen member and at the moment he entered her body she had to catch her breath. He was holding her hips as she rode him then she realized they were in motion. She had to tuck her head into his shoulder so he could see the road. There was no sense in putting anyone in harms way just because she wanted to suck his lips clean off of his face. He had put the truck in drive and they were headed for his house. He was flying down back-roads, while having sex with this beautiful woman.

"Good thing I live in the country with no neighbors, because this is the sort of thing that could definitely get people talking, or get you thrown in jail."

When he pulled into his driveway he pulled around back and held Ruby when he opened his truck door, before he got them out he reached over and grabbed her jeans and thong. "Ruby I am going to carry you in the house like this."

She wrapped her arms around his neck and said, "Let's go."

He climbed out of the truck with his jeans still on since all Ruby did was unzip him, and he carried her up the back porch stairs and through the back door and then through his kitchen. He was thinking about laying her down on the kitchen table but that would probably hurt her back so instead he went into his living room and sat down on the couch, holding her bottom in his large hands, since they were still connected. He hadn't pulled out of her; he didn't want to miss her warmth, not even for a second. He lightly bounced her on his lap while he kissed her, then she started bouncing herself and told him to hold still because she could do this. After a couple more minutes of this she came and then it was as if he could feel her release, because he came shortly after her. It was like an explosion and then they collapsed into each others arms. Without moving he whispered into her ear, "I love you and you are the sexiest mechanic I have ever seen." And without skipping a beat she whispered back, "I love you, too, you big sexy beast."

Chapter 6

After getting up from the couch and cleaning themselves up from their lovemaking Byron made sandwiches for lunch. They watched a couple of game shows on television while they ate and then Byron decided it was time to show her around his house and property. He lived on ten acres of land in the country. His house was a two-story log cabin with a wrap around porch, and in the front of the house on the second story there was a small balcony that came out from the master bedroom. There was also a small pond on his property and a trail through the woods that was used for riding dirt bikes and four wheelers.

She loved the setting of his house; she felt that it had an older charm to it. He told her the house had been in his family for the last four generations of Miller's. Since he was the only son of his parents, who owned the house last, it automatically went straight to him. When they finished touring the outside of the house he figured she needed to know the inside as well as the outside, the first stop inside of the house was the kitchen. She loved the fact that it had been updated very lightly; it had older butcher-block countertops and brand new stainless steel appliances. Besides the older charm, the house had a Tuscan feel to it, and it worked. There were iron plaques above the kitchen entrance and all through the house. The living room was immaculate with its red walls, tan furniture, and black wrought iron staircase.

After the complete grand tour Byron said, "I want to take you someplace where you get to dress up. How do you feel about that?"

"I would love to go, but I don't have any dressy clothes. Since I work at the shop so much, that really doesn't leave much time for me to have a social life. Until lately, that is."

"Let me explain, my job has me working at the local high school dance and I would love to not have to go alone. Do you think you could help me with that?"

"I would love to go with you, but like I said, I don't even own a dress."

"Not to worry, I have just the thing."

She was suddenly very curious, he never let on about what he did for a living, but she would soon find out. After they cooked dinner together and washed the dishes, they left his house and headed for town.

"Where are you taking me?"

"You'll see."

Forty five minutes later they pulled up in front of this cute little dress shop. The stores lights were off and the closed sign had been flipped.

"They closed at five," she told him. He grinned at her then pulled a key out of his pocket and unlocked the door. She looked at him with real surprise on her face.

"This is your shop?"

"I own the entire shop and the contents inside of it. I purchase dresses, gowns, gloves, tiaras, purses, jewelry, and other girly stuff directly from the designers and sell the stuff at a reasonable price to the people in town."

She began moving around the store, so he changed the subject.

"What is your favorite color?"

Her response was immediate, "Blue."

"Any particular blue?"

"No, just blue."

He began walking down the long lines of dresses and pulled two from the racks, they were both sapphire blue. In his left hand he held up a knee length dress with spaghetti straps and a matching shawl. In his right hand he held up a floor length ball gown, it was strapless and it had a slit in the front of the top that went to the center of the breasts. It also had little rhinestones fixed to the bodice. She couldn't stop looking at the ball gown, she had never really seen, let alone worn one before.

"You need to try them on and see if they fit you."

"I only need to try one on. I love the ball gown."

He showed her to the dressing room and helped her get out of her clothes and into the gown. When she saw herself in the mirror she wanted to cry.

"I feel like a princess, you made me into a princess. I feel so pretty right now." "Sweetheart, I am so glad you are finally seeing yourself how I see you; however you are so much more than just pretty. I think gorgeous, beautiful, and sexy all together don't quite cover it, but it's fairly close."

She smiled and said, "You really are too good to be true."

He decided now as the best time to ask her to the prom, since she was already dressed up. He took her hand and very seriously asked, "Ruby Pinkerton, would you please do me the honor of going to the prom with me?"

She could tell he was trying to be overly sweet with this, so she decided to play along. "Why, Mr. Miller, nothing would make me happier. Are we going to get drunk and have sex afterward like all the other hormonal teenagers do after prom?"

"Hopefully, if you want to."

After staring at herself for a few more minutes she decided she needed to change. She headed to the dressing room with Byron right behind her. She was reaching for the zipper of the dress, but he was already pulling it down slowly and kissing along her shoulders. The dress fell away to the floor and Ruby let Byron have his way with her. They had made love twice already today and tonight made three times, she still felt like she could take him again. She found her clothes in the dressing room and got dressed quickly as Byron pulled his pants back up from around his ankles and zipped himself up.

"The prom is in two days, and I'm sorry it is such short notice."

"That's okay; I have to work like everyone else."

"I have connections here in town because of all the women that shop here so you can get anything you want done. Just tell them you and I are together and I sent you. If there is a problem tell them to call me here. You can go and get your hair done, manicures, pedicures, and if you really want to, you can go to the tanning beds, but I like your skin the way it is. It goes just right against the blue of your dress."

"About that, how much do I owe you for the dress?"

"You already took care of that."

"I did, when?"

"In the dressing room. I don't let any of my customers pay me with sex, but for you I think I can make an exception."

"You are such a sweet man, where did you come from again?"

"I'm Bluffton born and bred, I was taught to play hard, except when it when came to women. But you already knew that. I'm a gentleman and I was raised to be this way, to take care of women, and since I don't have, or didn't have one for myself until now that is, I tried to take care of every woman that came through that door."

"I like the fact that you want me to belong to you."

"Really? Well maybe someday I can find a way to make that a little more permanent."

"Byron, you know I would love that."

Chapter 7

"Damn it! Dude, you are not supposed to be in the bay of the shop! You need to go wait in the office and I'll be right with you, or you can talk to Brad."

Stupid teenagers. The prom was tomorrow night and all she had on her mind was Byron Miller, with his perfect face and chiseled body. Since she was thinking about Byron so much she kept forgetting what she was actually working on. Then it hit her, that teenager that she was just yelling at worked at the parts store and came by to deliver the carburetor for the 1955 Chevy pickup that she had been working on. She ran into the office and got the carburetor from the kid and took it into the shop where the Chevy was sitting. She laid the heavy part on the back table and then went back to look into the engine compartment to remove the old carburetor. She was leaning way into it and had it almost completely free when she heard a long whistle. "Damn. Hey, baby."

She pulled herself out from under the hood with a glare in her eyes—whoever just whistled was going to regret it—until she could see that it was Byron standing in her shop.

"What are you doing here?"

"Well you told me bring my tire by here and you could patch it. Plus, I really like seeing you in action. You're so sexy when you are all greased up and dirty."

"Well I'm about to close so you get to be the last job of the day. But first could you help me get the tire out of the back of your truck?"

"Sure. Do you need help locking up?"

"No, I like to leave the doors of the shop open while I work so I can look out for the crazies. Besides, I have to patch your tire first and then we can lock up."

Very quickly Byron went to his truck and got the tire out of his truck bed and rolled it back to the shop where Ruby was waiting with what looked like an oversized needle and a black strip of leathery, greasy material running through the eye. The handle looked like a T-shaped gearshift for a car. He rolled the tire to her and she got a pair of pliers and found the nail and yanked it out, then she slammed that needle into the hole where the nail was and turned it about ten times and yanked the needle out cleanly. The strip stayed in the hole.

"Babe, that was pretty damn impressive."

"Thank you. Okay, I can put air in it, but that's about all I can do for your tire."

She rolled the tire to her air compressor and pumped it back up. Then she reached for the socket wrench off of her work bench and started rolling the tire back to his truck. When she got to the truck she laid the tire flat and got down on the ground underneath the truck so she could mount it back into its proper place underneath the truck bed. Byron noticed that she was struggling to hold the tire up so he crawled under his truck to lend her an arm and a shoulder, and maybe even a knee—if she needed it-for the tires support. She finished tightening the bolts in the bracket with her socket wrench and when the tire was in place underneath the truck she slowly started to roll out from underneath the truck, but Byron grabbed her arm and pulled her to him under the truck and kissed her. Byron broke the kiss he started and got out from under the truck then offered her his hand to help her up. She accepted it.

"You know Ruby, some day I am going to need to know how to change a tire and other small things that involve vehicles, would you be willing to teach me a few things?" "Well, since you taught me a few things that don't involve vehicles, I guess I could teach you a few things in return."

Byron's mind went right into the gutter; he hoped she wasn't just going to just teach him about trucks.

The next morning she didn't even open the shop, she figured she'd be all over town getting ready for the prom. She went and got a manicure and pedicure first-she had no idea how women wore these fake nails—then two hours later she had an appointment with a hair dresser. The lady at the beauty shop worked a miracle on her head. Ruby's hair was pulled up on top of her head and she had ringlets of hair falling all around her face. She thanked the lady and went to grab lunch. She was having Cindy help her get ready for tonight. She went and got a medium pizza with the works and headed for home. Ruby got to her apartment and found Cindy already inside waiting with a makeup case and lots of other girlie things.

"We need to eat before you lather all that gunk on my face."

"That's fine. I am so happy for you. Did you even go to your high school prom?"

"Yeah, we went, for like twenty minutes he didn't want to dance at all, and he said all the people being crowded together made him very uneasy."

"Oh honey, that sucks. So basically you missed your prom?"

"Yeah, pretty much. I'm okay though, when Byron found this dress for me he actually said and I quote, "Ruby Pinkerton would you do me the honor of going to the prom with me?"

"Wow, he actually asked you like that?"

"Yep."

"Well maybe you should plan on holding on to him."

"Cindy, I hope I never have to let him go. God help anyone that tries to take him away from me."

When they finally finished the pizza, Cindy got to work on Ruby's face. She really played up Ruby's eyes by adding a gold eye shadow with black eye liner and mascara. When she finished her masterpiece she said, "Oh my god, would you look at yourself and tell me what a miracle worker I am!"

"He's not going to recognize me; it's a good thing he knows what the dress looks like."

"You know, I was thinking, I have never seen you get all dolled up for anything . . . much less a man."

"It may sound corny to you, but when I am around him there are fireworks. I feel real chemistry between us when we are together. Cindy, he was my first."

"You slept with him already?"

Ruby looked at Cindy with goo-goo eyes and blushed then said, "I love him, and I know I made the right choice."

"Well sweetie, if you're happy then I'm happy for you. Okay, so what time is Casanova picking you up?"

"He should be here in about fifteen minutes. I feel nervous right now, just like high school."

"Ruby, you're what, twenty one, right?"

"Yeah, why?"

"What do you have to be nervous about? You are young, you have your looks which by the way can I say, damn, I am a magician, you are curvy and any woman in her right mind would kill for your body, you have your shop, you have your family, and you have me."

"I think I also have Byron."

"Well see, then you don't need to worry."

As promised Byron was at Ruby's apartment at seven o'clock on the dot. He knocked on the door and was surprised when someone else let him in.

"Hello, handsome! Wow, so you are the one that is changing my best friend up in a girlie way."

"Umm, yes I think that's me."

From the other room he heard Ruby say, "Yes honey, that would be you. I'm coming out and you better not laugh or you'll be going to the prom alone."

"Yes, ma'am."

Ruby stepped into the room and watched Byron as his breathing slowed down; he was really looking at her. Without really thinking about it he took a few steps toward her and reached out to catch her hand in his, then he lifted it slowly and kissed the top of her hand as he gazed into her eyes, then he kissed every knuckle on that hand. He had gotten a white rose corsage for her and he slipped it over her wrist after he kissed it.

"You look incredible, like some princess right out of a fairytale, but so much more beautiful."

"Thank you. You look very handsome, too."

Ruby went over to the coffee table and got his boutonniere and pinned it onto his jacket. She had also gotten him a white rose. With that they waved goodbye to Cindy and were headed out the door to the parking garage where Ruby spotted a black stretch limo in the parking lot with a man holding the back door open for them.

"I have never ridden in a limo before."

"That's good, because neither have I."

"Then why did you . . . ."

"I wanted tonight to be special for you, all the way up until when you wake up in the morning."

"Really, what did you have in mind?"

"You'll see, now lets go."

They were helped inside the limo and then they were off. Ruby very quickly took notice of how massive it was, it even had a stocked mini-bar. Not long after they were in motion Byron leaned toward Ruby and kissed her softly, then he pulled away and said, "There's more where that came from."

"How much more?"

"You'll see later, I promise. Do you want a drink before we get to the school?"

"Sure, how about a whiskey on the rocks."

"How is it a little thing like you can drink something as strong as straight whiskey?"

"I like it because it goes down warm, and you don't drink it, you sip it. Plus, if it makes you too hot you get to take off some of the clothes you would be wearing."

Byron was watching her sip at her drink and thinking, "God, she's hot." She was really like something right out of a male fantasy. They arrived in the high school parking lot around seven thirty and he said he was glad they were early, because he wanted to act like a teenager and make-out with his girlfriend in the back of their limo until the prom started. She wanted him all over her as much as he wanted to be all over her.

He grabbed her glass then set it on the table beside them and said, "Ruby, you are the most gorgeous woman I have ever laid eyes on. I want you right now, but I am going to restrain myself because I don't want to mess up your hair, make-up, or your dress." "Byron I don't know if I can restrain myself, you look so handsome in that tux. I feel like a real lady tonight and I want to thank you for that, the right way. So move a little closer and let me kiss you."

Byron had a grin on his face when he said, "Yes ma'am, I would love that."

He watched her close those bright blue eyes and open her mouth slightly as he bent down and she kissed him. She made the connection with his mouth and then his tongue. Their breathing was so hot and heavy that they were steaming up the windows. Their tongues were dancing against each other and Byron's hand had moved to cup her breast when a knock on the window scared them both. "Yes," Byron said.

"Sir, it is eight o'clock the prom is fixing to start."

"Thank you. We'll be just a minute."

Byron had to give himself a minute to come back down from his arousal. The door opened and Byron got out first and then helped Ruby out. As they walked through the gym doors Ruby noticed some females gawking at her and Byron, "What's their problem?"

"I have been chaperoning this schools prom for the last four years, so I would come by myself and dance with whoever was here alone."

"I find it hard to imagine you being here alone."

"They are so jealous of you."

"Why?"

"Because you are gorgeous and you're my date."

"Well, all I have to say is, you're mine and I do not share well with others."

"I am glad you feel that way, because I was hoping that we wouldn't be sharing anything with anyone."

They had a great time at prom; they danced, drank punch, and kissed when no one was watching. When prom was finally over he told her that he had a surprise for her.

"Oh yeah, what is it?"

"It's not an it, it's a place. We are going to your apartment for a minute. You need to pack a couple days worth of clothes and something to swim in."

"We aren't leaving the country are we?"

"Trust me, we are going to be teenagers tonight. We are going where all prom kids go afterwards. The Island. I have a house right on the water."

"Oh wow, really. I've never spent the night on The Island. This'll be great."

They were barely in the limo when Byron was kissing her again. As soon as the car took off she was working at removing his neck tie. When his tie was gone he was shrugging out of his jacket while she was undoing his shirt buttons, she wanted to see his sexy chest. She slid a hand over his pectoral muscles and giggled when he made them move. Then, she had yet another surprise for him.

"I can make my chest move, too."

"No you can't."

"Wanna bet? Unzip me and you can *feel* for yourself."

Ruby turned around so he could unzip the dress and when he had it done she turned back around with her eyes half closed and she took his hands and placed them on her breasts. She smiled at him then bit at her bottom lip and sure enough, Byron found out that she could make her muscles move, too. Suddenly he was very interested in seeing what other parts of her body she could make do interesting things. They arrived at her apartment and before the limo door could open to expose her he had her zipped up again, and he was trying to relax his mind so his erection would go down.

"Let's go and get your bag."

When she got inside her apartment she grabbed a duffel bag and Byron was coming out of her closet with nothing but lingerie.

"How did you find that stuff so fast? I had it hidden pretty well, I thought."

"Honey, I'm a man, I can smell skimpy clothes from miles away. I am going to lock you in the house, and make love to you every second of the time we're on the Island."

"Do you promise?"

They left her apartment and headed to the limo and Ruby was shocked when the limo was gone and instead Byron's truck was in the parking lot.

"When did you bring your truck here?"

"Before the prom. I told you I had plans."

Chapter 8

"Ugh, that was a long ride. I'm so glad I slept most of the way, now I know I won't be tired tonight." Ruby said as she and Byron walked in through the front door of the house at Pirate's Cove. They were holding hands and Byron was carrying their bags.

"Oh yeah, what did you have in mind, Ruby?"

"I plan to make love to you in every position that I can get myself into."

"Now that sounds nice and right up my alley, maybe I should go out and get a bottle of wine. Parties are always better with a drink or two."

"That would be great. Do you want me to come too?"

"No you can stay here I'll only be a few minutes. I swear I'll be right back."

He leaned down and gave her the sweetest kiss that had her wanting more instantly, but he pulled away and headed for his truck, then he was gone. Ruby locked the door behind him and turned to face the spacious living room and grabbed her bag and headed to the stairs to look for the master bedroom. When she found the overly spacious bedroom she noted in her mind that it was the last door down the hall on the right, just incase she got lost in this massive house. The room was huge and definitely masculine. There was no headboard or footboard on the bed, just a large king size bed that was raised off of the floor with a black comforter and white pillows and shams to match. She also saw the fireplace that begged for attention in the center of the left wall. It had white painted bricks and some black scroll design painted along the edges. This room looked like a picture out of Better Homes and Gardens. She saw the large doors on the right and opened the one closest to her and found the huge walk-in closet with the built in island centered in the middle of the room.

She placed her duffel bag in the center of the island and started pulling out various items and noticed now that the only outfit she packed, or that Byron let her pack, were her black leather pants and the black halter top. Other than that outfit she found two string bikinis and a lot of lingerie that she forgot she owned. She noticed that Byron had gotten sneaky and stuck a pair of her three inch heels in the side of her bag. She knew a lot of sex was going to be happening in this house over the next two days and now she couldn't wait to play dress up for him.

*   *   *

Byron hadn't wanted to leave Ruby hanging like that, with that kiss, but he had to run out for more than just a bottle of wine. He knew of a jewelry store that was open pretty late and he knew that he was ready for Ruby to be his. He really wanted to do the right thing and make an honest woman out of her. She was more than just a lover to him. After being with her as much as he had he knew there was no way he would willingly go back to being without her. That would be like having to stop breathing. It was something that he simply couldn't do in order to survive. He parked his truck outside the jewelry store and got out to see a closed sign. At that point he felt a little defeated. He was fixing to leave when a miracle happened, he saw someone moving inside. He immediately got back out of his truck and knocked on the door. A little old man with fuzzy white hair came to the door and said, "Sorry, were closed."

"Sir please, I only want to buy a ring, I am going to ask my girlfriend to marry me tonight. Please, I swear I'll only take a minute of your time."

The man gave Byron a puzzling look to say the least but gave in. "Oh, alright. Come on in." He unlatched the door and let Byron in then latched it back. The man turned to face Byron and asked, "Do you love this woman?"

"Yes, sir. I do."

"I just wanted to make sure you weren't jerking my chain, I get a lot of teenagers in here this time of year that have no idea what love is. I know they come here from their proms and they think they are in love, it's cute and annoying at the same time."

"That's not me, I swear. I haven't known my girlfriend long, but I already know that I can't live without her. Could you show me your engagement rings? I am looking for something that is elegant, like my Ruby."

"Her name is Ruby?"

"Yes, it's beautiful, isn't it? Why do you ask?"

"Well, there is this new fad going around. People aren't using plain diamonds anymore. Let me show you what I'm talking about. He pulled out a princess cut diamond surrounded by smaller rubies on a white gold band.

"That is gorgeous and I'll take it. She is going to love this. Thank you for opening up for me."

The man took the ring and placed it in a red velvet ring box then handed it to Byron. "Not a problem," the man said after swiping Byron's charge card, "I never get in the way of love."

"Well, I am very grateful. I really need to hurry back to Ruby."

"Good luck tonight."

"Thank you again, and take it easy."

He turned around and was out the door heading a couple of doors down to a store known as The Wine Cellar. They had a lot of wine to choose from, but he decided he would like to treat Ruby tonight. Instead of wine he got a bottle of Cristal. He went to the counter and charged his card again, and was finally on his way back to the house. He was so looking forward to seeing Ruby's face again, although he had only been gone for like twenty minutes. When he got to his house he decided to ring the doorbell and surprise her. She came to the door and sang out, "Who is it?"

"It's your sexy beast, please, let me in. Or I'll huff and puff and use my keys again."

"No, not the keys. Hang on just a second, sexy beast."

He could hear her giggling and unlocking the deadbolts and the slider lock and he realized that she didn't feel safe unless the house was on lockdown. He knew he would be the remedy to that situation.

As long as he was with her, no one would look at her wrong or lay a finger on her. Byron liked this feeling of being her masculine protector. He was happy he finally had someone that needed and wanted him around to be protected.

Ruby finally opened the door and he noticed she was still wearing the dress, but no shoes, and her hair was all down and curly. He thought she looked ethereal. She gave him that naughty little grin that he came to love so much, and his body gave his mind no choice. He leaned down and kissed her hard on the mouth, sucking her bottom lip ever so gently into his mouth. While, kissing her he slowly inched them further inside the door so he could set down the Cristal. When he found a solid surface all of two seconds later the bottle was down and his arms were around Ruby's waist. He pulled her to him until there was no space left between them.

She got her swollen lip back and bit his lip and he let out a low growl, and then said, "Oh, you want to play that game, huh? Sounds good to me, babe." Byron leaned down ever so slowly, letting the anticipation build and bit at her neck where he knew she liked it best. She let out a loud cry of pleasure and her goose bumps were back.

"I think I like this foreplay stuff." Ruby told Byron as he was kissing her neck. Then like an unwanted phone call her stomach growled. He couldn't help but giggle when he asked, "Do you want anything in particular to eat?"

"Nope, just you."

"Well you need food, and I can't fill up your stomach like I can other parts of you."

He was grinning at her when she said, "Whatever you want is fine."

"There's an Italian place close by that delivers, how about I order pasta and breadsticks." "That sounds great. How long do you think it'll take, I really want to take a shower and get out of this dress?"

"Take as long as you want. What do you say about eating in an hour?"

"That's perfect."

"Great, then go shower and I'll make the phone call. See you in a minute."

She kissed him lightly on the lips and turned and headed upstairs to the master bedroom and bathroom. The shower in the master bathroom had two shower heads, a built in bench, and glass walls. The rest of the bathroom included a two person Jacuzzi tub and twin sinks in the long vanity. She was starting to get used to all the massiveness. As soon as Ruby turned to walk away Byron had the phone to his ear telling someone on the other end who he was and what he wanted then he told them to have it here and ready in an hour. When Ruby made it to the top of the steps he was hanging up the phone.

She walked into the shower and turned on the water then turned and went to the closet to grab her bag of bathroom toiletries. It took a few minutes to locate her bag since she didn't unpack that bag earlier. When she found her bag and went back to the bathroom she found a sexy, naked man standing in front of her facing the mirror. He was shaving rather quickly. She had never seen a man shave before. It was really interesting, as he was wiping his face with the towel, on pure impulse Ruby placed a finger tip at the nape of his neck and slowly descended it; she watched all his muscles tighten. When her finger came to his waist he swiftly turned around to face her with a dreamy look in his eyes, but he was far from sleepy.

He was standing there in the bathroom nude for her with the most impressive erection he had ever shown her. Slowly she turned around and said, "Could you help me out of this dress." When he started unzipping, he remembered that she wasn't wearing a bra, and he was unzipping slowly because he didn't want to have a heart attack. When the dress reached the end of its track it simply fell down to the floor. His eyes widened a little and that low growl came back again, he got a little excited. He was excited because Ruby was naked underneath. He knew she had to have planned this. Then he remembered she didn't like underwear so maybe it was just that he was going to give himself a heart attack. Especially if he couldn't remember little tid-bits of information like that.

He lifted her up and out of the dress and then held her to him, he carried her luscious, curvy, and naked body into the shower where he sat her down on the built-in wall bench. He took his time as he washed and conditioned her hair. While the conditioner was setting in her hair he had a sponge all lathered up with her body wash that smelled like pomegranates. He washed her body starting with her neck, then her arms, slowly he circled her breasts, then he moved lower to her stomach, hips, back, legs and finally back up to her curvy bottom, which he took his time in washing. He then moved on to her mound which when he rubbed her there with that sponge she felt something, because she said, "It's your turn right after I get this conditioner out of my hair." He sat himself down and she shampooed his head and made a thick lather, while he massaged, kissed, and sucked on her breasts, she was enjoying the attention so much she even massaged it into his scalp with her fingernails.

When she finally had the shampoo out of his hair she conditioned his hair, and then lathered his sponge. His body wash smelled very woodsy, like cedar chips and orange oil on a rainy day. She started washing his torso first using her hands more than the sponge. She wanted to feel his muscles tightening when she rubbed sensitive spots. She washed the rest of him and saved his manhood for last because she wanted to give him pleasure. She said, "I think you're going to like this, but you have to tell me if I do something wrong."

"Babe, I don't think you could ever do anything wrong."

She lathered up her hands with the suds from the sponge and grabbed the length of him with two hands, and still needed one more. She started working his shaft slowly then more intensely. She had Byron groaning and cursing. A couple of times she heard him say, "Damn it, baby, please." She ran the water over him while still jerking and pulling on him, and when the bubbles were gone she lowered her mouth to his erection, but he told her no, she was too late, and he squirted his hot love potion all over her chest and stomach. He didn't do it on purpose and she knew it. He looked at her and said, "I'm sorry, I should have aimed away."

"No, it's okay."

"Well, come here anyway and let me clean you up again."

Her grabbed her sponge and body wash and lathered it up again in seconds and had her stomach and breasts cleaned again.

"Now it's my turn to torture you." Byron said.

He lifted her up again and had her standing on the wall bench and then he helped her steady herself as he placed her right foot on the mounted soap dish. He gazed at all of her and at that moment he couldn't help himself, he had to have her. He cupped her mound with his hand and found her wet. She was wet from the water, yes. But the wet he felt was hot and a little bit sticky and sweet. Her body was crying for release and he was going to answer that call. He traced the line of her tattooed treasure map and then plunged a finger inside of her and he heard her moan loudly at the same time her eyes rolled back into her head. He pulled his finger out and began licking and kissing at her clit. He was driving her out of her mind. She was bucking and thrashing and nearly fell a couple of times, but when he inserted two fingers into her sheath she screamed and pulled his hand away and said, "Byron, . . . I'm . . . coming." Byron didn't intend to move. She squirted him with her liquid and it got on his neck and chest. Instead of being disgusted or shying away he licked at her again, helping her come off of her sexual high. Slowly. She helped him clean up again, then they both got out of the shower and he pulled on a pair of boxer briefs and Ruby asked Byron, "What should I wear?"

"How about the red and black panties and one of my button up shirts, I forgot girls wear pajamas."

"I don't wear pajamas, I wear boxers and tank tops. Just like you."

Byron couldn't help himself, he was a gentleman after all, he held the shirt up so she could put her arms through the sleeves. He walked around her and buttoned only two buttons. The one right below her breasts and the one under that one. With the shirt being buttoned like it had been, it made him want her more. It wasn't tight underneath her breasts, but at the top of the shirt her cleavage could be seen from both sides. Damn she is sexy in my shirt, he thought as she followed him down stairs to sit in his lap in the recliner.

"When is dinner going to get here? I'm starved."

"Well, I would say in five minutes or less."

"Really."

"Babe, you just sit back and leave dinner to me, okay?"

Ruby gave a salute and followed it with a, "Sir, yes, sir."

A few minutes later the door bell rang and there was a delivery boy standing in the doorway. He was holding a paper bag that smelled like the Italian version of heaven. Byron noticed the kid trying to peek around him. So he would sway just enough to block the kids' view of Ruby. Apparently he really wanted to sneak a peek. He kept trying to look around Byron even though he towered over the kid. Byron gave the kid the money and an evil eye and told him to get lost. The kid said, "Hey, what about my tip?"

"You should have thought about that before trying to catch a peek at my woman."

He slammed the door in the kids face and turned back around and faced Ruby saying, "He was really eyeing you. I thought I was going to have to knock him down to size."

"Really? I didn't even notice him all I could see was a sexy beast standing at the door in his underwear."

"You stay right there and keep looking sexy and I'll get dinner separated and into bowls and I'll be right back."

"You sure you don't need any help?"

"No. No. You stay right there."

He was in the kitchen before she could think of a reason to argue with him. She could hear him clanging bowls and glasses and she decided she would tease him during dinner. She reached down and unbuttoned the top of the two buttons. Now there was no way he could get away without seeing some flesh. A few minutes later he returned to the living room with a tray and a look on his face that told her that he noticed the undone button. He proceeded onward towards the coffee table and put the tray down, then leaned over and gave Ruby a kiss and then kissed the swell of both of her breasts. On the tray was a plate of breadsticks, two bowls of pasta, two champagne flutes, and the bottle of Cristal. He was staring at her. When he finally broke the silence he was opening the champagne and pouring it into their glasses.

"Ruby I would like to make a toast. I love you and I hope to never be less than the man you want and deserve, and to a long and happy life. To us."

"I love you too, Byron, and that sounds perfect. To us."

They clinked their glasses and sipped their champagne.

"Byron I have never had Cristal, it is really good. You didn't have to go to extremes. I would have settled for Andre."

"No, you won't settle for Andre. I want to give you things and make you happy. I knew you'd like it, so I got it for you. End of story."

Byron handed her a bowl of pasta and a fork and told her to dig in and help herself to the breadsticks. She took the first bite of pasta and then reached for a breadstick. She grabbed the breadstick on top and then stopped with it in mid-air. She looked at Byron with tears suddenly filling her eyes and running down her cheeks and said with a shaky voice, "Is . . . that . . . what . . . I. thinks. It. Is?"

Byron took the breadstick from her and removed the ruby encrusted-and slightly crusted-engagement ring from the breadstick and got down on one knee beside her and said, "Ruby, I know we have only been together for a short time, but I feel complete when I'm with you. I love being around you and I can't stand it when you are not around me. I think you're perfect and you're perfect for me, like no one else has ever been. I have never wanted anyone as much as I want you. I swear I will love you until the day I die and possibly after that. Would you please, do me the honor of marrying me and making me the happiest man in the world?"

By the end of his proposal Ruby was actually crying. She climbed out of the recliner and sat on his risen leg and leaned into his neck and said, "Byron Miller, I love you, too. I would love to be your wife. Nothing in this world would make me happier." Byron took her left hand in his and kissed her ring finger on the hand closest to her heart and then slid her ring on and then kissed her ring, followed by the top of her hand. While still on bended knee he hugged her closer to him and whispered, "Thank you, you have just made me the happiest man alive. Oh yeah, and you're my complete fantasy. I didn't think that was romantic enough so I thought I'd just tell you after you said yes."

Chapter 9

Byron and Ruby spent one full day in bed, completely loving on each other and the next day downtown on the island attending Motorcycle week. That was a surprise to them both. When they saw all the motorcycles in town they went back to the house, and Ruby got to wear her leather pants and halter top. Byron thought she fit right in with this crowd. They went to a bar where a lot of the bikers were hanging out and got to see a lot of the different bike makes and models. She told an older man with a long white beard that she would rather drive her truck than a small bike. The man didn't take offense to her statement, but said you couldn't make him ride in a vehicle that looked like a cage.

By the end of the trip Ruby and Byron had met a whole slew of people, some of which actually lived in their area. A couple of the people were asking Ruby about her business and they promised to come by. All together it was definitely a good trip.

When it came time to leave and go home neither of them wanted to go. They had been having so much fun here. They packed their stuff up on Sunday evening and left that night. The trip seemed longer, but this time Ruby had something to do besides sleep. On their way off of the island she sent Byron into one of the local shop for a notebook and pens.

While she was riding home, she was going to be planning. They had decided to have a small ceremony; they didn't think they would quite have fifty guests. Ruby picked out the colors, blue and white. Byron told her the wedding could happen at the house so they wouldn't have to pay someone else for a venue. She liked his style. Byron decided on the pastor, it would be someone he has known all his life, his old friend Pastor Thomas. Ruby decided she would only have Cindy as her matron-of-honor, and Byron asked her if Scott would be interested in being his best man. They decided the wedding was going to happen in two weeks. They were sure that with the families help they could get this done and it would be phenomenal.

When they got back home they immediately called all the family members to tell them what was going on. Ruby called Cindy and told her about the wedding. She also asked if she and Scott would be the matron of honor and the best man. Of course they agreed, and invited Ruby and Byron out to dinner and dancing to celebrate. Dinner went quickly and then they went out dancing. Byron and Scott sat out for most of the dances while Cindy and Ruby danced to almost every song with each other. Byron surprised Ruby a couple of times when he pulled her to the dance floor and whisked her around to show her off. He could slow dance and he liked showing Ruby that he could sweep her off of her feet.

The first week of getting ready for the wedding was the craziest; Cindy and Ruby went everywhere to find the perfect dresses. They finally got what they were looking for on day five of shopping. Cindy's dress was a blue knee length dress with a plunge top, it looked gorgeous on her. Ruby also found her perfect gown or at least the one she knew Byron would like. It was a corset topped dress with a ball gown flare at the bottom, it was almost the exact style as her prom dress. He liked that dress so much that she figured, why fix something if it isn't broken. Cindy was losing her mind along with Ruby, because the men were going out on their own to pick out their tuxedos and didn't want the girls to know what to expect. That worried Ruby a little bit, but then she remembered what Byron did for a living and thought, he would know what looks good on him better than I would.

It was Saturday and Ruby and Byron had made a date at the coffee shop.

"Wow, babe you look beautiful. I feel like I haven't seen you in days."

"That's because you haven't, we've been so busy, running here and going there. I swear I'm going to lose my mind."

"Ruby, I am so happy that we're doing this quickly, I can't wait to officially call you my wife, Mrs. Miller."

"You could always practice saying it."

"Yeah, I know. I don't want to think about going through another week of this without seeing you. My family is crazy, your family is crazy. No offense."

"None taken."

"We could elope."

"Babe, the guests are going to be here next Saturday, and the caterer has already been paid. It's just one more week."

"You're right, you're always right, it's just seven more days. I'll deal."

"Okay now, babe, Monday is my final fitting for my dress, Tuesday I get to figure out how I want my hair, Wednesday I start packing up my apartment, Thursday I have a doctors appointment, Friday I go and get my nails done, and Saturday is supposed to be the night of the bachelorette party, but I said I didn't want one. Since I don't want a party I will be free on Saturday night, so Mr. Miller, can I spend the evening with you?"

"You told the girls you didn't want a party? Wow. I told the guys I didn't want one either."

"Why did you do that?"

"Well, I don't need to see some strange woman wearing things that I want you to wear in order to appreciate what I have for me right here. Now babe, why didn't you want one?"

"By now you should know me well enough to know that I don't like seeing naked men unless I'm engaged or married to them. Now can I spend the day with you or do I have to call the spa and schedule something?"

"You can come to our house and I'll turn it into a spa. How does that sound?"

"Great, but sweetie please, don't go all out, I want to relax."

"Of course, love."

On Sunday one week before the wedding Ruby and Byron decided to get away from everyone and go out. Or at least that's what they told the family. They ran outside trying to escape before anyone wanted to tag along. When they got inside Byron's truck he turned to Ruby and kissed her then with a very serious look in place, asked, "Why didn't you tell me you might lose your shop?"

"Well, because it hasn't happened yet, and I didn't want to worry you. Plus, I figured that if I did lose the shop I could help you at the dress shop doing whatever needs to be done."

"No way, Ruby."

"Well, I know I don't know much about dresses, but you don't have to be mean about it."

"I didn't mean it like that; I mean I won't let you lose your shop. I know how happy that place makes you and it makes me happy to see you happy."

"Hang on, who told you about the shop anyway?"

"Umm, Cindy. But don't get mad at her, she wasn't spreading gossip. She heard you on your cell the other day when you went shopping and she said that she knew you wouldn't tell me."

"It's true, on both accounts. They want to foreclose on my shop, and I know I have way to much pride to ask for help. I would rather live on bread and water and rub two pennies together for heat."

"Well honey, I don't think it will ever be that bad for us."

"I hope not. I'm sorry, I should have told you. No more secrets, I promise. Now are we going to just sit here, or are we going somewhere?"

"Well you can choose either the bar or the movies."

"I don't know, what's playing at the movies?"

He gave her a grin and said, "Who said we would be watching the movie."

"The movies it is."

When they got to the theater there was a movie playing that was in Spanish and they figured that would be just fine. They sat in the top row in the far corner, so no one could see them. When the movie started, they were very surprised to be completely alone, but not upset. The groping and kissing lasted throughout the whole movie, and when the lights came on they were surprised by how wild they looked. They went to the separate bathrooms and fixed their clothes then met in the lobby. Byron still had his eyes half closed when he got back to Ruby. He leaned close to her ear and said, "I need you tonight."

"I want you, too." She whispered back.

Byron decided he knew a place where they could go and there would be no interruptions. They went to the truck and headed to the beach. Byron kept a blanket in his truck for just this occasion. He had been hoping to get to make love to Ruby on the beach before, but time never allowed it. He carried the blanket down to the sand dunes and laid it out. Ruby was never one for public indecency, especially since she was only a few weeks into having sex, so she told Byron that she wanted to keep as much of her clothes on as possible. He told her that was fine, especially since she found a skirt to wear. Ruby unzipped Byron and pulled him out of his jeans while he was kissing her face and neck. She loved it when he was gentle with her. He reached a hand up her skirt and looked at her with his evil grin and slanted his head.

"Didn't you wear panties?"

"Yeah, but I took them off at the movie theater."

"Why didn't I notice that?"

"Because you were being sweet and trying not to expose me."

He kept his hand under her skirt and began to rub her until she felt friction.

"Byron, I'm ready for you." she whispered.

"That was fast."

"I already came once at the movie theater. That was the other reason I had to take off my panties."

"Good to know."

He pulled Ruby into his lap and let his shaft enter her wet spot. He started grinding into her and she loved every minute of it. Then he switched positions on her, he picked her up and had her on her hands and knees, he wanted to enter her from behind. She started to protest, but quickly realized that she liked this position, although she could feel that he liked this position more. He got to look at her bottom while he was thrusting himself into her. He came quickly and she didn't this time during sex, but she had once earlier. She figured it was because she was thinking too much.

When he finished, they laid on that blanket on the beach while the sun was setting. Ruby loved to look into his eyes when the sky went orange and pink. It really made his bright blue eyes pop. They were laid alongside each other when he leaned over her and kissed her gently on the mouth. Ruby knew how that kiss would end and said, "You can't possibly want to go again, not yet."

"Oh yeah, and why not?"

"Well, I think I got some sand in my crevices. I need to take a shower. You could join me, you know."

She hadn't really even finished her thought when he was standing up, and telling her, "Let's go and maybe we can sneak in."

"Where are we going to go?"

"Let's see, some of your family is at your place, some of my family is hanging out at my place, the beach house is too far away, wait I know, doesn't your shop have a shower?"

"Yeah, sort of."

"Then let's go there."

They got back to the truck and climbed in. Byron fired the engine and they were in motion. They didn't talk at all on the way to the shop; she figured he was thinking of new positions to get her into. She had never thought about christening her shop but now she thought that it would be fun. They had however christened her apartment, his house, the beach house, his shop, and his truck just to name a few.

When they arrived they got out and Ruby walked to the door and unlocked it and let them in. She of course turned around to lock it back behind them and that's when Byron scooped her up in his arms and was taking her to the garage part of the shop, he wanted her on the counter, on a stack of tires, all greased up, but mostly he wanted her in that truck she was rebuilding. Ruby reminded him she needed to use the bathroom first and he put her on her feet in front of the bathroom. Since her shower at the shop was mostly a water hose and cold water she opted against it and told him she had an alternate method. Ruby opened the bathroom door and when she went inside she pulled the door shut behind her. She grabbed some hand towels and soaked them in warm water and cleaned herself up. Byron found his way to the old Chevy trucks passenger door and surprise, it was actually unlocked. When Ruby was finished she walked out into the garage and found Byron standing next to the Chevy with droopy eyes and he was smiling at her. He walked up to Ruby and scooped her up into his arms again and carried her to the passenger side of the truck. He laid her on the seat and she scooted in until her head was at the steering wheel. At that moment Byron wanted her, he freed himself from the confines of his jeans, he was in a classic vehicle and didn't want to ruin the mood with extra foreplay, he was already way past aroused.

He made soft sweet love to Ruby in that truck and nothing could ruin the moment, not even the phone that was ringing in the office. When Byron was finished and satisfied with his love making to Ruby he pulled out and with a tear in her eye, she said, "You were so gentle. I like it when you are like that with me."

"I'm glad you liked it. It can be like that whenever you want it to be. Who do you think was calling here at this hour?"

"Probably one of the family members, they may be looking for us."

"Well then I guess I had better get you home, we don't want them thinking we ran away. Do we? Do you want to run away?"

"You are awful! No, we are not running away. Now why don't you come back down here and kiss me some more, you big softie."

"If I kiss you like I want to, I promise you won't be able to call me softie, big yes, but softie, definitely not."

"Byron, I really love you, you know that?"

"You show me that you love me everyday. I really love you, too. I am never going to be lonely again, and you can't imagine how happy that makes me."

"Yes, I can. I am never going to have to make a date with myself again. Which by the way always brought me down. I hated going places and seeing other people paired off, I never thought I would be good enough for anyone. I felt like my insecurities would always get the best of me. From what happened when I was a teenager, I always considered myself dirty, broken, and just emotionally damaged goods. I could always pick out the perverts in a crowd, but that night at the bar after I punched that jerk, and you defended me, I felt wanted and safe. I hadn't felt wanted or safe in such a long time before that moment. The moment you told him to apologize to me, I knew I wanted you."

Byron was looking at her with a thoughtful expression, then he said, "Ruby you hit him so hard that if I hadn't jumped in and grabbed him, he probably would have tried to hit you back. If I had known you back then when that rat-bastard came around I would have broken his legs. He never would have made you feel dirty, broken, or like damaged goods because you are none of the above. You are gorgeous, sexy, loving, sweet, incredible, and mine. I defended you because I love you and I'll be damned if he was going to hit you back or even think about it."

"Did I even thank you for that?"

"Not really, but you don't need to. It is my job to take care of you now, and I plan on being very good at that job. When that guy grabbed you in the bar, I wanted to haul him outside and teach him a lesson, but you beat me to the punch, literally, and I figured if I got sent to jail for killing that loser you wouldn't have a way home."

"Well I'm glad you didn't go to jail because the moment you grabbed him was when I realized that I wanted all of you, all to myself, that night."

Byron leaned over and hugged her to him then kissed her long and hard and said," Finally, I found my love, and she's got a mean right hook. Seriously, when did you learn to hit like that?"

"My teenage years. I went to school with a bunch of guys that always had my back and I called every one of them bubba, because they were like the brothers I never had. One of them gave me a quick lesson when I was seventeen; I have only had to use that weapon twice. She pulled away and said, "I saw you first. Who was that girl a year ago anyway, you never said."

"Well, we never dated she was more of a client. The couple of days you saw us together we were picking out bridesmaids dresses for her wedding party."

"Oh, I was just curious. If I was a cat I would be dead already."

They got out of the truck and walked back to the front office area of her shop to see who called. It was her mom just seeing where she was, nothing was going on, she was just curious.

"You ready to take me home?"

"Only if you really want to go."

"Never, but we really should go or they are going to try to start calling all the little drive through wedding chapels in Las Vegas."

"You're right. Let's get out of here. Will I get to see you tomorrow?"

"Well tomorrow is my final fitting and you can't see me there. So maybe tomorrow night. I told my mom I would hang out with her a little so I am cooking at my apartment you can come by and eat with us if you want to."

"Of course I want to, I'll be there."

Now that they had plans again they left the shop and Byron drove straight to Ruby's apartment and walked her to her door, kissed her long and hard and then disappeared back down to his truck. He couldn't wait to see her again tomorrow.

When Byron got home two of his cousins were there. He knew they were there to visit and one of them managed to find one of Ruby's thongs and held it up and said, "Dude, I found this in the couch! I can't believe you got the goods before you went on your honeymoon?"

Byron said, "Clearly you haven't seen Ruby yet."

Byron walked over to him and snatched Ruby's underwear out of his hand and said, "She's irresistible, and if you touch her underwear again, I'll break your fingers."

He felt bad about threatening his cousin, but thought, well at least I said it with a smile. He took her thong to his room and shut the door behind him. He wanted her here with him, but they were trying to make their families believe that they were waiting. It was harder than it should be. He took a shower and then got into bed wearing the boxers Ruby loaned him the night he stayed at her place. He was out in minutes thinking about only one person.

Ruby got inside her apartment and her mom was there curious about where they had gone. She told the truth, they went to the movies, her mom didn't ask which one or if she even liked it, so she didn't even have to lie. Ruby went to her bedroom and closed the door, all she wanted now was peace and quite, and a bath. She found her lavender bath salts that Byron had used the first time he took a bath here. She missed him, she sat in the tub and thought about all her plans over the coming week and came to the conclusion that they were crazy to try and get married next week. It was going to happen, but it was still crazy. When she finally got out she was all pruned just like Byron liked her, she went into her closet and found his boxers that he left from the second sleep-over at her place. They were softer than hers and they held his scent. She pulled on a wife-beater then went and got into bed on his side so she could find his scent on her pillows. It wasn't hard to locate the pillow he had used last time, it smelled like aftershave. She loved the smell of his aftershave, more so when he was wearing it. She fell asleep while holding his pillow tight to her chest and throughout the night she never let that pillow go.

Chapter 10

"It's Monday." Ruby's mother said as she busted her way into Ruby's room.

"God mom. What time is it?"

"Seven thirty, what time do you have to be at the dress shop?"

"Nine o'clock and it only takes me thirty minutes to get there."

"Then you should get up, plus someone is here to see you."

"Who would be coming here to see me?"

"Get up and go see."

Ruby didn't want to move but she managed to pull herself out of bed and made her way to her living room.

"Hey there, I just thought you would like some breakfast and coffee before you went to your final fitting."

Byron.

She just stood there, she was so happy to see him.

"Mom, could you give us a minute."

Her mom turned the corner and disappeared into the kitchen with the coffee cup and paper bag that Byron had brought by. When Ruby knew her mom was gone she ran across the room to Byron and jumped into his arms. He held her there by her thighs and they kissed intimately, until her mother came back in the room and said, "Can I . . . . fix you anything to eat Byron?"

When Ruby heard her mom's voice she turned to her and gave her a look that could melt ice.

"No thank you, Mrs. Pinkerton, I just know how Ruby likes to skip breakfast most days. Since she is going to be busy today I thought I should help her out in any way that I could."

Now he was looking at Ruby and said, "Eat breakfast, go to your fitting, and I'll see you tonight at five thirty."

"You're going to work?"

"Well, one of us should."

"Ha Ha."

He kissed her this time as he lowered her to the floor. When he broke the kiss off, he said, "Remember, I love you."

Then he turned and was out the door. Ruby's mom looked at her in shock.

"Wow, if your father ever kissed me like that I don't know what I would have done. I like him Ruby, he's a keeper."

"Yeah mom, he definitely is."

Ruby went back into her room and got dressed she decided to wear something comfortable. She put on shorts, and a t-shirt, and she found a pair of flip flops. When she was ready to go she grabbed her heels for the wedding dress and headed out the door. She didn't want anyone going with her. The main reason being that she didn't want anyone to see her tear up when she tried on her dress. When she arrived at the dress shop at eight forty-five the woman still had a girl in the back, so Ruby had to wait a minute. The bride that was here first apparently gained a size and her wedding was in a month. How sad, Ruby thought, she had never had that problem, she never had to go on a diet or eat a certain way to maintain her figure, she got to eat whatever she wanted and in mass quantities. The other woman's hysterical crying broke her train of thought and she walked to where the girl was sitting. The girl in question didn't look very big but she was still in her dress and the saleswoman was telling her that they had plenty of time to let it out a size and there was nothing to worry about. The girl was upset, but she got out of her dress and changed back into her clothes and was on her way.

The saleswoman came around the corner and said, "You must be Ruby."

"Yes."

"Come on back, your dress is ready."

Ruby was so anxious. The first time she tried the dress on it was so big, they had to clamp it in the back to see what the front would look like. The woman told Ruby to go into the dressing room and strip down to her underwear and call her when she was ready. Ruby thought to herself, thank god I wore underwear and a strapless bra today. Ruby called the woman in and the woman had her dress set up in the middle of the room like a teepee. She told Ruby that she would have to step into it. Ruby very lightly stepped into her dress, then the woman was behind her pulling it up around her. When she had the corset top around her chest, the woman unhooked Ruby's bra from behind with one hand. Ruby was shocked for a second and then thought; yeah you might be able to see back of the bra. The woman was pulling the laces in the back of the corset and very slowly Ruby's cleavage was starting to rise out of the top of her dress. When the woman finished tightening the laces, Ruby had to hold her breath. She was shocked at how pretty she looked. She knew that when Byron saw her in this dress he would want to peel it off of her.

"It is perfect. Byron will love it."

Ruby loved the dress it hugged her curves and showed off her assets. She started spinning around and looked in the mirror while she twirled. She was beautiful, and she felt it. "Okay, that's enough, I need to take it off before I ruin it."

The woman started untying the laces and Ruby just stood there holding back tears. She couldn't wait to see Byron and tell him how much he was going to like the dress. The saleswoman helped her back out of the dress, and then Ruby got dressed and met the woman at the sales counter.

"How much do I owe you for the alterations?"

"Aren't you marrying Byron Miller?"

"Yes, why?"

"Well, he called this morning and gave me his credit card number so it has already been taken care of. That was okay wasn't it?"

"Well, I guess so. How did he find out where I was getting my dress altered? Cindy!"

She thanked the woman and headed out the door wondering how she managed to get a generous man on top of what he already was to her. She refused to open the shop this week since she was so busy with the wedding. She still had to go by the florist today and make sure she could still get her flowers, and then she had to go the store and get all the ingredients for her wedding cake that her mom was making, and the ingredients for tonight's dinner. She was making lasagna tonight and she only needed a few things from the store. She got to the florist and she was in luck, they still had the flowers she wanted. She asked the woman at the counter if they could make two bouquets one larger than the other with the blue hydrangeas, and the white daisies. The woman told her sure and asked when she needed them by. Ruby told her someone could come by and pick them up on Sunday morning. The lady at the counter told her that was fine and then asked her name.

"Ruby Miller."

She gave her name very proudly. She figured she would be the one to pick them up so what did it matter if she gave her Byron's last name. She left the flower shop thinking about how great the bouquets were going to look against Cindy's dress and then her own. She climbed into her truck the same as everyday and was headed to the grocery store.

She grabbed a buggy when she got to the store and waltzed in through the electric doors. She was in such a good mood that nothing could get her down. She pulled her moms list from her bag and started hunting for all these different cake ingredients.

Cake: cake flour/ vegetable oil/sugar/eggs/shortening/
confectioners sugar
Dinner: noodles/meat/sauce/ricotta/mozzarella

It took some serious looking, but she finally found everything on the list and headed to the cash registers. She got to the check out counter and started pulling stuff out of her buggy and the cashier was ringing it all up and the bagger was keeping up with her. They had a good rhythm going. When she heard the total she almost fell out, it was a good thing she had a secret stash in her wallet. She paid the cashier and got her change. As she was getting ready to walk out the door the bag boy was walking beside her and asked if she needed any help. Ruby thanked him then said no she could handle it. When she got to her truck, she saw him leaning up against the outside of the building watching her. It made her a little uneasy but she told herself it was nothing, he was probably just looking at her truck. She loaded her groceries into the back seat floor boards and made her way back to her apartment.

She called her mom on the way and asked her to meet her down in the parking lot so she could help her unload. It was about four-fifteen when she got home so she was very surprised to see Byron's truck in the parking garage, where he usually parked. She parked her truck and her mom and Byron came through the parking garage doors to help her. She realized she really liked all this unexpected attention she was getting lately. Byron was at her side in a second and greeted her with a sweet little kiss. He started grabbing bags and only left two, Ruby handed one to her mom and she grabbed the other one. They made their way upstairs and when they got inside the apartment Ruby's mom took all the cake ingredients and set them on the back of the kitchen counter. Ruby and Byron unloaded everything else, dumping it into the fridge. Byron said, "Hey Ruby, can you come with me, I need to show you something on my back. Mrs. Pinkerton, we'll be right back."

Byron led Ruby to her bathroom and then locked the door behind him. Byron pulled Ruby in close and put his mouth right next to her ear and whispered, "Ruby do you remember how you jumped at me this morning and how I held you up?"

"Yeah."

"Do that again."

"Really?"

"Uh, huh."

Ruby backed up a few steps then ran at Byron and jumped back into his arms. Byron caught her and held her by her butt this time, gripping it in his wide capable hands. She leaned in to kiss him and he pulled away saying, "You don't know what you did to me this morning. When I set you down I was hard, and I didn't want your mom to see anything so I had to leave really quickly."

"I was wondering why you didn't wait for me to say, "I love you."

"The moment you jumped into my arms I became rock hard. I wanted to lean you up against the front door and take you right there, but your mom was in the room and I thought that would be somewhat wrong."

"Well, yeah, I'm glad you waited, but how do you feel about a quickie right now?"

"I'm a man. Naturally I love quickies. I love making love to you, no matter the time limit."

He began kissing her and then leaned her back against the door and said, "Your bathroom door will do."

He set her down, and started pulling at her shorts and panties, while she was taking off her tank-top and her strapless bra.

"Wow!" Seemed to be all he could get out of his mouth. He reached down to his pants and unbuttoned and unzipped them, then he pushed them down to his ankles. When he looked up Ruby was in mid-air and she landed right on top of his erection. She let out a squeal of delight and he had her pinned up against the door, driving himself into her heated core. Byron spent the next three minutes kissing her while he pounded into her soft spot. She was so light it wasn't really a problem for him at all to hold her up. At the moment before he came, he looked her in the eyes and said, "Ruby . . ."

She moaned into his ear when she felt his liquid coursing through her body. She was stunned. Never before had he said her name during his release, this small notion warmed her from the inside out.

"We better get back out there before my mom gets really curious."

He nodded then slowly pulled himself out of her body. She watched him clean up while she put her clothes back on. He really was something to look at. Byron had just buttoned his pants when she heard her mother coming down the hall. She knocked lightly and said, "Ruby is everything okay?"

Just for show, Ruby grabbed the back of Byron's shirt and yanked it up so she could pretend to look at his back, then she opened the door.

"Yeah mom, we're fine he had something on his back, but it was easy to "get off." She looked at Byron and he smiled at her double meaning of those words. They left the bathroom with her mom right behind them asking, "When are you going to start dinner? I'm starving."

"As soon as I get in the kitchen. Now go sit down and watch something."

Her mom was trying to be helpful and said, "I could help."

"No, Mrs. Pinkerton, that's okay, you go relax. I want to help my wife."

Ruby's mom smiled at her then left the kitchen. Ruby and Byron spent a long thirty minutes in the kitchen preparing dinner and they would get touchy when her mom was shouting at the television. Even a few kisses got passed around, behind her moms back, which made her feel like a sneaky teenager. She liked it. After they finished dinner, Ruby and Byron did the dishes together and then they snuggled together on the couch for a movie that neither one of them intended to watch. Sadly, the movie ended and Byron and Ruby got up off the couch and were walking to the door when he said, "I have to work tomorrow, but you can come by if you want to."

At this point of their conversation Ruby's mom was standing in the kitchen doorway watching her daughter closely. Because Byron knew Ruby's mom was watching he leaned down and kissed her tenderly while she was wrapping her arms around his neck. Her mother turned red and left the room. Mission accomplished, he thought to himself. Since Ruby was still kissing him he lifted her a little bit so she was on her tip toes. He didn't want to stop the kiss, but if he didn't he was really going to make her mom blush. She didn't want him to break off the kiss either; she was really getting into it. He felt himself hardening beneath his khaki's and he knew it would be harder to hide in these pants than in jeans, so he stopped the kiss and looked at Ruby then glanced down. She followed his gaze and said, "OH! I'm so sorry, honey."

"Don't apologize. I like that it's this easy with you. I like it that I can just look at you and want to take you right there. I just wish I didn't have to go. But I know I will see you tomorrow right?"

"As far as I know. Nothing should change between then and now."

"Good because I might need your help getting something off the top shelves at the shop. I might have to hold you up." He gave her a wink and she caught on, now. He was throwing sexual content in her direction and in a way that would leave her mom in the dark.

"Really, like what a clothing "rod" or a "mound" of dresses?"

"I don't know, possibly both."

He pecked her on the lips and said, "I love you, you little tease," right into her ear.

"I love you, too babe. See you tomorrow."

Chapter 11

The next morning Ruby awoke like she did the previous morning, holding onto his pillow and wearing his boxers. She hated being away from him, and truthfully she could probably cool down her sex drive a bit if he was here. But being away from him just made her want him more. As soon as she rolled over she was thinking about what she had to do today. She knew she had to get her hair done and then she told Byron she would come by the shop for some afternoon delight. Her appointment at the salon wasn't until ten so she had about an hour to kill. She got out of bed and pulled her hair up into a messy bun, and went and jumped in the shower. When she got out she put on her black see through bra,-that Byron liked so much-with her low cut blue jeans,-that came just above her pelvis-and one of his long sleeve button up shirts with a wife beater underneath it. She thought she looked sexy enough. She let her hair down and didn't worry about make-up. She was going to a salon for god sakes. It was their job to make her look gorgeous.

Enough time had passed when she decided to leave her place, that there was no way she could be early or late. She grabbed a Pepsi out of the fridge on her way out the door, locked the door behind her, then headed for her truck. When she got outside she half expected Byron to jump out and surprise her. She wanted to see him again, and her mind and body were in agreement with each other.

She got to the salon and signed in, she was fixing to sit down when she saw a hair book and snatched it up. She sat cross legged in the crowded lobby and thumbed through it. She found a style she liked, but the color was a little different. She decided she wanted to try this look out first and then if it didn't look right the woman could do whatever she wanted to her head. When they finally called her back, a process that seemed to take forever, the woman put a drape on her and Ruby showed her the style she wanted. The woman looked at the style then at Ruby and said, "Yeah, I can do that. Did you wash your hair today?"

"No."

"Okay, follow me please."

Ruby got out of the chair and followed the woman back to the sinks where she washed and conditioned her hair. Ruby loved scalp massages, and that was what this felt like. The woman led Ruby back to her station and said, "By the way, I'm Lilly."

"Nice to meet you Lilly. I'm Ruby."

After shaking the woman's hand Ruby sat down and the woman got to work blow drying, combing, and tucking hair. She finished Ruby's hair in less than an hour, and when she turned Ruby to see her hair, she was in shock. She said, "Well, I would have never known my hair could do that."

"That's what I'm here for."

"Could you do my makeup as well? I would like to try to pick out a look for my wedding."

The woman went and got her make-up kit and came back. Ruby told the woman that she had no idea what would look good against her light skin. The woman said, "Don't worry, I've got you covered." She hummed to herself as she worked a miracle on Ruby's face. When Ruby got to see herself she noticed the blush on her cheeks was very light, her eyes looked smoky, and her lips were a luscious blood red. She knew Byron would want to kiss her everywhere, when he saw her today. She thanked the woman and paid her at the counter then made her way out the door. Before she made her way to Byron's shop she went to the Chinese restaurant on the other side of town and got takeout, sesame chicken and white rice with Chinese vegetables for two. When the order was ready she was all grins as she left and got into her truck. Ruby started driving to his shop and then the craziest thing started happening, her truck started stuttering and then it shut off right as she got into the grass. Ruby popped her hood and got out of her truck. She climbed up her tire and got under the hood and started moving her battery wires around, but nothing happened. So Ruby was left there, stuck in the middle of town and no way to get the truck to the shop unless she called her sexy beast or a tow truck. She didn't want to bother him at work but she really had no choice, she wasn't going to be the female mechanic that called another mechanic. She called Byron and told him where she was and not to worry, but her truck had broken down and she was stranded. He immediately wanted to know what was wrong and he said he would be right there and they could use his truck to tow hers to her shop. He was not lying, he got there in about ten minutes, and it usually took about fifteen minutes. By the time Byron got to Ruby she had one end of her chain wrapped around the tow hook on the front of her truck and was heading towards the back of his truck to hook the other end of the chain to his hitch. He really liked watching her work, and the fact that she was willing to work in makeup with her hair done really blew his mind. She was like no one he had ever met before. He watched her in complete amazement and when he realized she was in his truck waiting for him, he got in and they were off. When they got to her shop they pulled her truck through the garage and shut both doors then went into the office. She placed the food out on the table and he fixed her plate, and took it to her and then he fixed his and they began eating and talking about what could be wrong with the truck. When they were done she went into the shop to see what the problem was. Little did she know, her Knight in Shining Armor was right behind her watching her every move and calculating every step she made. She realized she never asked him if he liked her hair and makeup, and thought that after she worked on her truck if she was still clean, and her hair was still holding up she would ask him what he thought. She looked back at him and noticed he was gawking at her while he was standing on her ladder.

Her truck was so big that there was no way she could just look under the hood. She actually had to climb the front end or the tires like a monkey or climb up a ladder to get under the hood of her truck. When she finally was at the top of the ladder-a whole four steps-she lifted her leg and sat on the edge under the hood. Byron got to the top of the ladder and looked down at the motor and whistled.

"Wow! There's a whole lot of stuff in there."

Ruby couldn't help but laugh at him. He was so cute and honest. She loved the fact that she knew about something that he didn't have a clue about.

He looked at her in complete amazement. She knew exactly what she was doing under her hood. She was all dolled up and looked like she was supposed to be getting married to him, today. He loved that she wanted him to see what she looked like, what she would look like, she wanted his opinion. He also loved that she could look so amazing while doing some dirty work, and she wasn't afraid to get a little grease under her nails. All the other women he had ever known were a little more uppity and would have died at the thought of crawling under a hood.

After searching for a little while Ruby said, "I found the problem."

"Really? Babe, that was fast, it would have taken me an instruction manual, a tutor, and a month to figure something like this out."

"Relax; it's just a dead battery. I can have it replaced in minutes."

"You are so sexy when you talk shop. Do you realize that?"

"Are you trying to make me blush? If you are, it's working. Mechanic's aren't supposed to blush."

"Yeah well, the last mechanic I went to, before you graced me with your presence was a hairy, sweaty, fat man with foul breath. You on the other hand are a gorgeous, made-up, and sweet smelling mechanic. And you kiss well, too."

"As soon as I replace the battery and clean my hands up you can show me how good I kiss."

"How about I show you how good you kiss right now?"

"Okay."

Ruby took a greasy finger and ran it down Byron's cheek and said, "Got you."

"I'm gonna get you for that. You better run, girl."

There wasn't much room to run in her shop, but she could run around her truck just fine. She took off toward the back of her truck intending to climb up and into the bed but he caught her by her waist, turned her around, and pushed her up against the truck.

"You shouldn't have done that, love."

He grabbed her leg in his hand and lifted it to his waist. He started kissing her hard; he wanted to devour her right then. There between their bodies, Ruby could feel Byron becoming erect.

"What are you thinking about right now?"

She asked him that same question after she fixed his tire and he couldn't resist her. She was hoping for that same reaction again.

"I'm thinking that your truck bed is almost as big as a normal bed. I am also thinking that if I have you on top of me, you won't hurt your back. But mostly I'm thinking about your soft skin and how sweet you smell. I could eat you up starting from down there."

She gave him his favorite devilish grin and asked, "So what's stopping you?"

Without saying a word he started unbuttoning her shirt at the bottom, working his way up while he kissed at her neck and chin. She was trying to work at his pants, but she was getting nowhere. He kept backing away. When he had her shirt completely unbuttoned he opened it wide and saw her wife beater and felt defeated.

"I don't think I can get that over you hair without messing it up."

"Then why don't you just rip it off of me. You are my sexy beast after all."

He wanted to see what she was wearing for him today. So he grabbed two handfuls of that cotton material at the bottom of her t-shirt and ripped it right up the center.

"Damn, love, that even felt sexy."

"Now, I feel like you might actually eat me."

When he saw the black bra his mouth was instantly busy, first he kissed her softly at the swell of her breast, then he moved down to nibble at her nipple through her bra. She started moaning loudly, she was so turned on right now. This was their second time in her shop and it was getting to be just as good as the first time. Byron grabbed her shirt from behind her and threw it into her truck window. He didn't want her going home looking dirty. Next he unbuttoned her jeans.

"You may want to do yours first."

"Why?"

"Because, I have on one less layer than you do."

"Damn, love, that's hot. Now your jeans are definitely coming off."

He lifted her up so she could climb into the bed of her truck and he was right behind her. He sat down in the middle of the truck while she stood right in front of his face and he began unzipping her tight, low cut jeans. He couldn't get a grip on the jeans because they were so tight so she had to help a little. She had them pushed down to the top of her landing strip, when he saw their position he groaned long and hard right into her belly. He grabbed the sides she had pushed down and was yanking them off with all he was worth. He wanted to see her completely naked in front of him, on top of him, and with him inside of her. He lay back on the floor of the truck bed and said, "Babe, I need you to come a little closer." She took a step in his direction and he pulled her on top of him. He began kissing her again and this time he had his hand on her butt, slowly he touched her most sensitive spot and then he plunged two fingers into her unexpectedly and she screamed out a loud pleasurable squeal. She was trembling at this point. Byron knew she was primed and ready and he couldn't wait to give her what she needed, and wanted so badly. Instead of him making the next move, Ruby jumped up and said, "My turn to make you scream." She looked at him with her eyes slanted and then licked her lips in anticipation.

"You ready for this, big guy?"

"Yes, ma'am!"

Now that she had his approval she reached down and unhooked his button and unzipped his jeans and helped him out of his shoes and his socks. His boxers were on, but they never really did their job, and she decided not to mess with them. She reached down and grabbed a whole hand full of this gorgeous, sexy man beast that she had full control over. He lay back with his hands locked together behind his head.

"Babe, I'm primed and ready, so you don't need to do too much."

On that note she leaned down and kissed him where it counted and began licking the length of him. That did it, Byron's shaft was standing straight up and he told her he wanted her to sit in his lap. He picked himself up and sat up against the back glass with his knees up. Ruby came closer to him and climbed into his lap, Byron was holding his shaft waiting on her sweet warmth to envelope him. He was literally aching to be inside of her right now. He guided her onto him and when he penetrated her, her breath escaped her. She loved that he could do this to her. She looked at Byron with that devilish smile and those twinkling, sleepy eyes and said, "I'll take it from here." He grabbed her hips and held on as she rode him hard. It took a little longer than usual for him to blow, but Ruby had no problems. He wasn't upset that she had gotten off faster; in fact he was relieved that she got that much pleasure that quickly. She was really grinding into him when he said, "Ruby, here . . . I . . . go . . ." Right after saying that, he held her down on him while he blew his load. She could feel it; she loved it when he exploded into her, that was also when she could feel him pulsing inside of her. After his release he pulled her close to him and held her for the longest time. They both sat there in the back of her truck greasy and dirty and together.

"Your hair is all messed up. It was beautiful while it was intact. Your make-up was sexy, too."

"I can see the color of my lipstick clearly, now."

"You couldn't see it before?"

"Yeah, I saw it, but it is nothing compared to now, I can see the lip prints all over your neck. Byron can we stay here awhile? I'm not ready to be away from you, not just yet."

"We can stay here as long as you want. I still have the blanket in my truck from the beach. I'll be right back, don't move."

Byron pulled his jeans on then jumped down out of the truck bed and ran out of the garage. Ruby sat there alone in the back of her truck with her arms wrapped around her knees. She still hadn't gotten dressed yet, and didn't plan to. Byron ran back in the garage with the blanket in his hands and reached into her truck to get the shirt, then climbed into the truck bed. He positioned himself behind her and wrapped her shirt then the blanket around her shoulders. He was holding her tight and she said, "I can't wait until I never have to leave your side."

"Ruby, since I laid eyes on you, you have never had to leave my side. I would never turn you away."

Chapter 12

It was Wednesday afternoon and Ruby found herself at her apartment still filling up boxes with everything she could get her hands on. She started packing around six this morning. She got home at two am and found her mom gone already. Her mom was going to stay with Cindy for the rest of the week so she wouldn't be in the way while Ruby was packing and moving to Byron's house. She was also supposed to make the wedding cake over there.

She had just finished writing *kitchen stuff* on two more boxes when she heard a knock on the door. She wasn't expecting company today, but she wasn't going to turn it down either, especially if they wanted to help. She opened the door and standing there was her sexy beast, he had Cindy on his left side and her husband Scott on his right side. Scott was holding two pizza boxes. Byron said, "I located some extra help."

"You guys don't have to help me, this place is a mess."

"Actually love, I think you and Cindy are going to be packing boxes while Scott and I load it all up."

"Well alright then, come on in, honey." Byron let the others in first then walked in slowly and kissed her eagerly, like he hadn't seen her in a week, it had only been about eight hours. When he broke the kiss off he asked, "So how much have you gotten done?"

"Well the living room, bathroom, and bedroom are packed. All that's left are the kitchen and my closet. I started in the kitchen already, but I'm scared to tackle my closet. I don't think I have enough boxes."

"Well, that's what I'm here for."

Cindy had already started filling boxes in the kitchen so Ruby grabbed two empty boxes followed by Byron who also grabbed two boxes and they headed into her closet. Byron managed to somehow get all her shoes into just two boxes, for completing that small task she kissed him. She was so amazed by him. Byron opened a closet drawer and shouted, "JACKPOT!"

"Oh, crap, I really thought that I had hidden that stuff a lot better."

"Guess not. Now why don't you wear this stuff? It's sexy. I would love to peel it all off of you or you could play dress up or model it for me, I'm not picky."

"Okay fine, just dump it all in that box and tape it closed."

Byron started pulling more stuff out of the drawer and couldn't believe his eyes. See through teddies, fishnet tights, a corset with a matching thong, and four different costumes. She had lube and toys and then he found an instruction manual which showed a picture of a sex swing. His mouth dropped then he looked at her while she was packing up clothes.

"Tell me, do you still have this swing, or did you throw it out?"

"I still have it, its right there in the back of the closet. A girl friend gave it to me and I have never had a reason to use it."

"Oh, we are so taking this to the house."

"Fine, but can we finish packing first I really want to finish before my doctor's appointment tomorrow. I want to go see him with no stress."

They finished packing up the closet pretty quickly once Byron stopped looking for sexy stuff.

"Let's go grab some pizza, then Scott and I can finish loading up and we'll go to the house and unload it again. When did you tell the landlord you'd be out by?"

"I told him I would be completely out by Sunday. Now, I'm hungry what did you order on the pizza?"

"Your favorite, I ordered it loaded."

"Thanks, babe. That's so sweet."

They got into the kitchen and saw Cindy and Scott were eating pizza out of one of the boxes already. Ruby went to the fridge and grabbed four sodas and passed them around. Everyone was sitting crossed legged on the floor, due to her dining room table and all other furniture already gone.

"Hey guys, how's the wedding stuff going? Are you nervous yet?"

"Cindy, the wedding is going to be very smooth, the two families are working together and that has left me with just a few things to take care of. If I didn't have all this help how would I manage to get married after only being engaged for two weeks? And, no I am not nervous, at all. I am right where I am supposed to be, with exactly who I am supposed to be with. I'm extremely happy."

Byron watched her as she spoke and he felt the love she had for him floating in the air, he wanted to cradle her in his arms, but he settled for a kiss instead, since Cindy and Scott were still in the room. Cindy was quiet for a moment as she stared at Ruby and Byron; she realized she really had never seen Ruby this happy before or as relaxed and she couldn't help but smile.

"Ruby, I really wish you would reconsider the party."

"No way, I am going to relax at home, besides, Byron has already promised me a massage, and a few hours of sleep and . . . more relaxing stuff."

"That sounds nice I know you'll enjoy it."

They finished eating, then finished loading up the trucks with the help of Cindy and Scott. Everything was completely loaded and the apartment was empty. Ruby wanted to walk around her old apartment one last time. Byron grabbed her hand and walked with her. She had been living on her own since she was eighteen, and this was her home. Sadly she would miss it, but she was happy that she would be living with Byron.

Everyone piled into both of the trucks and headed to the Miller house. When they pulled into the driveway Byron backed up to the back door and told Scott to back up front door. They started unloading Scott's truck first since he and Cindy had to go and pick up their kids and take them to softball practice. When his truck was unloaded they hugged Ruby and Scott shook Byron's hand and then they left.

"Alone at last."

"Babe, whatever you're thinking about doing to me, hold that thought; let's unpack your truck first. Then afterward we can relax or do whatever it is you're thinking about."

"That sounds promising. What you are doing? Are you telling me you promise to let me have my way with you?"

"Byron, I promise to let you have your way with me. Just as soon as you help me unpack some of the boxes."

Byron helped Ruby put boxes in the appropriate rooms and Ruby quickly realized that unpacking the boxes was easier than packing them. When they finished unpacking half of her boxes and all of her shoes and clothes she literally passed out on couch.

"Ruby, where did you go?"

Byron had just finished putting her extra sheets in the laundry room and was looking for her, but it was like she just disappeared. Then he heard her light snore and followed it to the couch. She looked so peaceful, laid out the way she was. Byron went upstairs to their room and cleaned off the bed and pulled back the covers. He made his way back down stairs and scooped his sleepy woman off the couch and carried her upstairs. He knew she was tired because she never moved, or stopped snoring. He laid her on the bed and covered her up, and then she rolled over and tugged the covers up to her chin. Byron stood there and watched for a while. He really knew he loved her, no woman could hold his attention like this woman could, and when she had it there was nothing else on the planet that mattered. He shoved the clothes off of his side of the bed then pulled his covers down too. He decided first he had better go and lock the house up and turn off all the lights. When everything was off he made his way back upstairs and stripped down to his underwear and climbed in bed right beside Ruby. She must have felt the movement because she snuggled even closer to him and threw her arm around his chest, she never woke up and he refused to wake her up whether she made him a promise or not. He leaned down and placed a few light kisses all around her face. Then he settled his lips on hers and lightly kissed her and said, "I love you, sweetheart."

Chapter 13

Byron woke up around seven and remembered the gorgeous woman right next to him. He rolled over and she was gone.

"Now, where'd you go?"

Byron jumped out of bed intent on hunting down his soon-to-be bride. His jaw almost hit the floor when he got downstairs to the kitchen and saw Ruby standing next to the stove scrambling eggs wearing nothing but a pair of lacy boy shorts underwear that had her butt sticking out.

He let out a long whistle and said, "Baby . . . . damn!"

He said it slowly and then made a high pitched whistle in her direction.

"What? What is it?"

Byron caused her to blush bright red, she could feel it and he could see it. He liked it.

"It's you. And what you are doing to me right now, just by standing there."

Ruby could see what he was talking about; he was rising right out of his shorts, again.

"Well, I was going to start a new tradition of making breakfast in the morning. I was going to make it fast and have it upstairs before you woke up. I can't believe my plan failed."

"If you make breakfast looking like that then neither one of us will get anything to eat and no one will be able to go to work. I am glad I ruined your plans if it means I get to see you like this."

"Point taken."

She looked down at herself, and understood. She gave him a grin then turned back to the stove and started working at the eggs again. Byron made his way behind her letting her know how he felt right now. He intentionally pressed his erection into her bottom. She felt it and pushed backed easily. She knew he was worked up and she was the cause, but she didn't need to make love right now. She was supposed to be at the doctor's office soon.

"I really hate to do this to you babe, but do you think you could wait until tonight? I still have my doctor's appointment to go to this morning."

"Yeah, I guess I can wait, but if I have to wait could you put a shirt on so I don't accidentally jump you from behind."

"Sure, I'll be right back. Could you watch the eggs?"

Ruby ran upstairs and grabbed one of Byron's long sleeve button up shirts that was long enough to cover her butt. She was walking downstairs while buttoning and met Byron in the entrance to the kitchen.

"Do you realize that you could be wearing holey sweats and I would still want you? I don't think my shirts are helping the cause. I am going to go take a shower and then I'll come back down and eat with you."

"Okay, babe. Don't use all the hot water, please. I want to take a shower, too."

Ruby got to the stove and found two plates and divided the eggs up, giving Byron a little more than her, since he-of course-had the bigger appetite. Ruby was lost in thought about her new life. I am in my kitchen, in my house, with my husband, and he thinks I'm gorgeous. I really don't think life could get any better than this. Ruby was finishing up her eggs when Byron appeared at the bottom of the stairs dressed for work. His work clothes consisted of dress slacks and a button up shirt with a t-shirt underneath. He was dressy without being dressed up.

Ruby kissed him when he got into the kitchen and then Ruby went upstairs to take her shower. She got out and went into their closet and found her comfy sweats and a stretchy t-shirt. She ran back into the bathroom and pulled her hair up into a messy bun and put on some light makeup. She was ready to go.

Ruby kissed Byron at the back door of their house and headed for her truck and then the doctors office. Since Ruby had replaced the battery in her truck, she hadn't had a single problem with it. She figured it knew better at this point in the week.

Ruby pulled into the parking lot at her doctor's office and jumped down out of her truck. When she walked in the front door she instantly heard little babies crying, and smaller children running around. These kids were so cute, but obnoxious. She went to the counter and signed in and then went and found a seat.

God I hope I don't need anything that requires needles, Ruby thought while waiting at the OB/GYN office. She had been there thirty minutes and had already urinated in a little plastic cup for the urine test. She wondered what could possibly be taking so long this time. After about ten more minutes of thinking that something was wrong here the nurse stepped out and said, "Ruby Pinkerton, please follow me." The nurse took her to the scale and weighed her. Ninety-five pounds, now there was a shocker. Then she checked her temperature and her blood pressure, all were normal. The nurse led her to a small examining room and grabbed one of the dreaded paper dresses and told her to change out of her clothes and leave her socks on if she'd like. Then she turned and left the room. A few moments later there was a knock on the door and her doctor came in. He sat on the stool across from the examining table and said, "Ruby, we didn't remove your IUD did we?"

"No, why did it fall out?"

"Actually, Ruby it seems you may have done the impossible. You are pregnant, honey. Congratulations!"

Ruby went totally pale and still, then her doctor saw the tears. He took her hands and said, "Ruby, I need to do an ultrasound to see how to address this situation."

"O-OKAY."

"Is there someone I can call for you?"

Ruby nodded to her doctor and pointed to her purse. He quickly handed her the purse and she began hunting her cell phone. She immediately started scrolling through the contacts until she found Byron's number. She hit send then handed the phone to her doctor. She didn't trust herself to tell him what was happening without completely breaking down. She could hear Byron on the other end.

"Hey babe, what's up?"

"Umm, this is Dr. Toroya, I'm Ruby's OB/GYN. I'm here with Ruby and she asked me to call you."

"Oh my god, what happened? Is she okay?"

"She's alright, she just needs you to come down here."

"I'll be there in like five minutes, please Doc tell her that I love her and I am on my way."

"Will do, see you in five."

Five minutes later Byron ran through the door and was pointed in Ruby's direction by the nurse at the front desk. He opened her exam room door and ran right up to her and said, "Honey, what's wrong? I swear I was having a heart attack the whole way here."

"My doctor said my IUD got bumped or something and some of your swimmers got past it and now I'm . . . . pregnant. They want to do an ultrasound to see how big it is. They don't know if I should have it or if they'll have to remove it."

Ruby started to cry, and Byron looked at her and held her closely and asked, "What are the risks if you carry it full term?"

"Byron, I don't know, and I'm scared to death."

"Well, right now we are going to worry about you. I love you, and I'll worry about everything else once I know you're fine."

It took Byron a little while to calm her down.

"I'm sorry Byron, I don't know how it happened."

After a couple more minutes, the doctor came in with his ultrasound machine. Byron stood up and introduced himself to Dr. Toroya. Dr. Toroya told Ruby she was very lucky and then he told Byron that he was also very lucky, because he was going to marry the best mechanic in town. Cutting the chit chat, Dr. Toroya looked at Ruby and said, "Okay I need you to lie back for me." He reached down and parted her paper gown just over her abdomen, and said, "Now this gel is cold, but it won't hurt. Are you ready?"

Ruby looked up into Byron's eyes like she was afraid, and he could see it, so he answered for both of them.

"Yes, we're ready."

The doctor squirted gel on her belly and then began rubbing the probe back and forth over her belly. He asked, "Ruby when was the last time you had a period?"

"A few years maybe longer."

Byron answered for Ruby and she just nodded.

"Well, I think you must have conceived fairly recently, because there isn't even a heartbeat yet."

"Is that a good thing? I mean is it okay?"

"Yes, Byron everything seems to be okay. It is not a tubal pregnancy, so some of your mighty little swimmers just got right through her protection. I would like to consider personally, not medically, that this a sign that you are ready for a baby."

"Thanks Doc."

"Don't thank me yet, I still have to remove the IUD, we don't want it harming the baby in any way. I am glad it worked though, she had it in for four out of five years, and no real periods in at least three years. She's my favorite patient."

Ruby gave a little grin to the doctor but still didn't move. Doctor Toroya pulled out the stirrups and helped her get adjusted in them, then he opened a drawer that held a heating pad in it and all of his speculums on top of it. He dug around in the drawer trying to find the smallest one. When he found it he lubed it up and inserted it into Ruby while she squeezed Byron's hand, then he clicked it the dreaded three times. With each click her grip got tighter on Byron's hand. Dr. Toroya reached down and found a pair of long tweezers, stuck them inside of her and yanked the IUD free.

"Okay, kids, I got it. Now your baby should be fine."

Byron thanked Dr. Toroya and then Dr. Toroya looked at Ruby and said, "Ruby you can get dressed now and go home, take it easy for a few days though, and let your body catch up to what has just happened. If you start bleeding at all call me or go to the ER. They know how to get hold of me. Oh, and you can still have sex if you are up to it, if you feel tired though, don't do it." Ruby finally spoke in a whisper and said, "Thank you Dr. Toroya, but do you think the baby will really be okay?"

"I think as long as you take it easy and no strenuous exercise or lifting heavy objects your baby has a fighting chance."

Ruby smiled at the doctor and Byron freed one hand from around her body and shook his hand and then Dr. Toroya turned around and was gone.

Byron stared at her for what seemed like hours and was startled when she broke the silence.

"Honey, I didn't want you to leave work to come with me originally, but when he said I was . . . . pregnant, I actually believe I went into shock for a few minutes."

"Sweetheart, I'm glad he called me, I want to know when something is going on with you. How else will I know if I can help or not. Besides, that's our baby in there, growing, and I am so happy right now that I don't think you realize what you have given me, even if it wasn't a planned gift. I thought I was complete with having you, and I am, but now I get more, a new little miniature version of you and me. That is what I consider as love." He leaned down and kissed her softly then gently rubbed a hand over her belly then leaned down and lightly kissed her belly.

"Our baby is in there, and he or she is going to come out perfect, Ruby."

Chapter 14

Byron couldn't wait to get Ruby home, he was so excited, he was going to be a dad. That would make Ruby a MILF, a Mom, I'd, Like to, uh Fornicate with he thought to himself. He helped her to his truck in the parking lot and lifted her up into the seat. He didn't want to take any chances on Ruby being over strenuous. He knew she had been doing things on her own for so long and lifting heavy objects was something that she was used too. But for the next nine months she wasn't going to lift anything.

He drove her home and when Byron parked the truck he asked her sit still. She didn't move, she thought something was wrong until he came to her side of the truck, opened the door and lifted her out. He carried her over the threshold of the house and went and put her on the couch. He tugged her shoes off and found her a blanket and said, "Ruby, I am going to go get Scott so we can bring your truck home. Do you need anything? Want anything?"

"Babe, I think it's a little early for cravings, but you could get me a soda out of the fridge and pass me the remote."

He turned to the kitchen and disappeared inside the fridge. When he returned he had her soda and a bag of chips. Then he went to the recliner and found the right remote and handed it to her.

"Do you need anything else? I don't want you moving too much, until Dr. Toroya says we are out of the woods."

"You are so sweet babe, I love that you are worried about me, but stop, I am just as worried about the baby as you are and I'm not taking any chances. I promise you, I will be right here on this couch when you get back. Alright. Now go get my truck, please. And by the way, we love you."

Byron's heart should have melted; he loved her, and their baby, who technically was not even a baby, yet. He leaned down and kissed her softly and said, "I love you both, more. I'll be right back."

With that last sweet sentiment he was gone. As soon as Ruby heard him pull out of the driveway, she turned on the television, she wanted to watch one of those baby shows that are always on. When she found one she became totally into what was going on. She saw the mom before the pregnancy, during the pregnancy, through the delivery which in this case was natural birth, and afterwards when the loving mother was holding her little bundle of joy and tearing up from being so happy. Ruby was tearing up too; because this was the sweetest moment she had ever witnessed that had nothing to do with her. When the show was over and she was out of soda, she decided to take a nap.

Ruby could see a perfect little girl in her dreams. She had reddish brown hair with big soft curls like Ruby's; she also had the same heart shaped face. Her lips were full and a pale pink like Byron's. This was their child. She was dancing barefooted in Ruby's dreams. She looked like she was around three. She was wearing a white dress with lace added in the trim work. She was gorgeous. The most interesting thing about this child were her eyes. She had sparkly, sapphire blue eyes. She had to be their child. Their beautiful daughter.

Byron got home about and hour and a half after he left. When he came inside with Scott and Cindy right behind him he noticed that she had kept her word. She didn't move off of the couch. She made herself stay still. She was asleep. He walked over to her quietly and whispered in her ear, "Honey, I'm home. Scott and Cindy wanted to come by and see you. Do you need anything?"

She was whispering in her sleep. That was new. "Pretty, blue eyes." She kept saying it over and over. Byron went to her ear again and said, "Ruby, what's pretty, blue eyes?" Her response threw him for a loop, because she was still sleeping he wasn't sure that she had even heard him let alone that he would even get an answer.

"Baby girl."

Byron was squatting beside her, but when she said "baby girl," he fell to his knees. He wanted to cry he was so happy. He kissed her forehead and left her alone to finish her dream. Scott and Cindy didn't want to wake her either so they said they'd come back when she was more alert.

Ruby slept all night not even waking to eat, which had Byron a little worried to say the least. But reluctantly, he took Ruby upstairs and gently laid her out on her side of the bed and crawled in on his side. He pulled her warm body to his and kept a hand on her stomach at all times. She moved a couple of times during the night, but ended up getting really comfortable laying almost directly on top of him.

Two days later Ruby could feel the warmth of the sunshine on her skin and she rolled over on Byron's side of the bed and noticed that she was alone. She looked at the alarm clock, it was ten o'clock.

"Babe, where are you?" When she didn't get an answer she got out of bed, slowly, and went straight to the kitchen grabbing a banana as she walked to the back door to see that his truck was gone. Her doctor's appointment had been two days ago and she was doing great, no bleeding, no lifting, and Byron drove her to and from her nail appointment yesterday.

"Oh, today is spa day." she reminded herself out loud.

She went to the fridge, pulled out a cucumber, and cut off two slices for her eyes, and two more for her to munch on. Then she made her way upstairs to her bathroom and turned on the water for the Jacuzzi tub. She filled it with warm water and added her lavender bath salts, and a dollop of bubble bath that smelled like roses. Now she was looking for a face mask scrub. She found the pack in the back of her cabinet. She quickly layered the gunk on her face, avoiding her eyes, mouth, and nostrils. She unbuttoned her teddy-that Byron had given her-and it dropped to the floor like it weighed hundreds of pounds she stepped out of it and into the tub. She laid back, stuck her I-pods ear-buds in place, and put the cucumber slices over her eyes. The first few songs that played were lullabies and that helped her to relax. She was still a little sleepy so she decided a nap would probably help. She leaned her head back on the edge of the tub and simply fell asleep.

Byron was a little upset when be pulled back into his drive way and parked in his usual spot. It was Saturday, his shop was closed and yet somehow that woman found his number and asked him to open up just for her. Of course he went, but he still couldn't figure out why he went. Oh well, he thought as he got out of the truck, I'm home now, and I'm not working again for two weeks. He made his way up the steps to the back door unlocked it and went inside.

"Ruby, where are you? Love?"

No answer. When he didn't see her down stairs he immediately went to their bedroom, still no Ruby. He was fixing to panic when he went into the bathroom and saw her. He couldn't quite fight the giggle that came through his lips. She was surrounded by bubbles, she had green gunk on her face, cucumbers for eyes, and her hair was piled on top of her head. He realized she couldn't hear him so he went to the backside of the tub, and got right behind her. When he pulled out her ear bud he nearly scared her to death, but he whispered, "Honey, I'm home," into her ear. He couldn't see her eyes from the cucumbers, but he could see that she was smiling. Then she puckered up, she wanted a kiss and he was going to give her what she wanted, no matter what she looked like. He leaned down to kiss her and when he did she rubbed her face into his.

"Ewww, what is that stuff, it tastes gross."

"It's not guacamole. You don't eat it."

"Oh."

"It's a mask; I'm cleaning out my pores."

"Well, I like the way your face looks without the mask."

"Thanks babe, that's sweet. Will you hand me that towel? I have been in here for a while, I'm all pruned."

"Why don't you just put on your robe? It's spa day remember."

"I remember, why do you think I was in the Jacuzzi with this gunk on my face. I was relaxing."

"Good, that's what you are supposed to do. Now, why don't you clean the rest of that awful gunk off of your face and put on your robe. I can give you a massage in a couple of minutes. I want to get comfortable, too."

Ruby went into her closet after she finished cleaning off her face and put on her robe and tied it loosely around her. She went into the bedroom and laid across the bed to receive her massage. Byron came out of the bathroom wearing nothing but his boxer briefs.

"I get to relax, too."

"So then why don't we relax together?"

Ruby sat up on the bed and pulled her robe down around her shoulders, so they were exposed. Byron was grinning at her so she thought she should give him a massage first. She took her fingertips and trailed them down his chest, when they got to his nipple she gave him a little pinch. He sucked in a deep breath. She kept her fingers going; she went down his thighs and all around his groin before stopping right where he wanted her to. She was holding his shaft in her hand while she leaned up to kiss him. He met her halfway and with both hands he untied her robe the rest of the way and took it off of her, letting it fall to the floor. He placed one hand on each of her breasts and their tongues continued moving in each others mouths, searching and exploring.

Slowly he pulled away and said, "Ruby, are you sure you want to do this now? The honeymoon is tomorrow. I mean it's not like we could do anymore damage, but . . . ."

"Not on your life."

Ruby pulled him back to her and they locked lips again, he lowered Ruby down onto the bed and then he moved lower nibbling at one of her nipples while his hand headed straight for her promised land. When his hand was cupping her he looked into her sapphire blue eyes as he drove two fingers straight into her sheath, he loved her reaction to him. She took a deep breath and held it while her eyes rolled into the back of her head. She was suddenly caught up in a rip tide of climactic emotion when she said, "Byron . . . . please . . . . now . . . . make love to me . . . . now."

Byron knew by her voice that she was where she was supposed to be so he pulled himself out of his shorts, pushed them off, and kicked them across the room. He knelt onto the bed right over her and settled himself there with one forearm on either side of her head. He then drove into her all the way to the hilt and she let out a pained cry. He immediately looked into her eyes and saw tears. He pulled out and had her in his lap in seconds, saying sorry over and over. She whispered, "I'm okay, really, it just hurt a little. Plus, Dr. Toroya said I might start crying a lot lately."

"Are you sure I didn't hurt you or the baby?"

"I'm fine, and I'm not bleeding, so I am going to guess that the baby is fine, too."

Without moving too much she lifted herself up and while still sitting on his lap she slid his shaft into her sheath, from the moment he entered her again, she was moaning. He was trying not to think about how he hurt her, because she wanted a release and frankly so did he. She was bucking her hips against his and he had her hips in his hands guiding her up and down.

"Oh god, Byron, just like that! Yeah, I'm . . . almost . . . there . . . ."

In the moment of him hearing how into it she was they came at almost the exact same time. He kept himself inside her during his release but she had no choice, her liquid was all over her thighs and southern regions.

"Aww man, I have to clean up again. I'm all gross."

"Well by the time you get out of the shower I'll have lunch ready."

"Okay, I'll be right back."

She ran to the shower got in and cleaned up and was out again. When she went down to the kitchen in her robe Byron looked at her and said, "Damn baby, did you even get wet? Lunch isn't quite ready, but how do you feel about left over spaghetti?"

"I think it's the best, especially when you made it."

He walked across the kitchen towards her, wrapped his arms around her and said, "You know this is like a fantasy of mine."

"What is?"

"You. And the fact that you are barefoot and pregnant in our kitchen."

"Babe, that's going to take some getting used to. I can't believe I'm going to be a mom. I am definitely going to have to work on that."

"You'll get used to the idea and you'll be a great mom. I know these things," he said it with an honest smile. Then he asked her a very honest question.

"Love, we never talked about this because I figured it would be a year or so after we got married, but how many little versions of us would you want running around the house?"

"How many do you want?"

"Well, I was thinking two. It's perfect because they would have each other, plus we can't have just one because I don't want him to feel lonely like I did when I was a kid."

"Aw, honey, I'm sorry you were lonely. Two is a great number, let's shoot for that."

He kissed her again and said, "No man on earth is as lucky as I am right now, I get to have you and our baby all to myself. Oh, have you told anyone that we're expecting?

"No, I figured we could wait until a week after we get back from the honeymoon to tell everyone."

"That sounds like a good plan that should keep us out of trouble, momma."

Chapter 15

They went through the rest of the afternoon talking about babies and she couldn't help but notice how excited he was with all the baby talk. They had already decided on two names that they really liked, if it was a boy, they would call him Mitchell Holden, and if it was a girl, they would call her Hailey Lynn. She hoped deep down that it was a girl; she wanted someone to doll up and make cute all the time. She also wanted Byron to have his son, someone that he could take hunting, fishing, and teach him how to ride a bike. Byron did say, "I don't care what the sex of the baby is, as long as you pull through, and it pulls through with ten fingers, ten toes, two eyes, and maybe an extra appendage."

They ordered dinner in again and ate quickly since they needed to sleep. They had to be up pretty early in the morning to get ready for the wedding. Ruby got in bed on her side still wearing her robe, and Byron got in bed right behind her, cuddling close to her. When he wrapped his arm around her waist Ruby rolled over, looked him in his eyes and said, "Byron, I love you, and I can't wait to spend the rest of our lives together."

This pregnancy was making her insides crazy because she started crying, again. Byron started rubbing her tears from her cheeks and he was running his hand through her hair.

"That helps, you know." Ruby said.

"What helps?"

"When you play with my hair, it feels good and it makes me forget why I'm crying."

"That's good to know. I love you more than you could possibly know and you'll find out how much tomorrow after the ceremony."

With that being said he kissed her lightly and said, "Good night, sweetheart." Ruby rolled back over and Byron held her close as they drifted to sleep one last time as two separate people.

It was about a quarter until four a.m. when Ruby screamed in her sleep and jerked herself upright holding her stomach. Byron sat up right beside her asking what was wrong. He started telling her she was okay, and that she was home and nothing bad was going to hurt her. She was hysterical. Byron noticed her holding her stomach and said, "Oh my god, what's wrong? What happened? Are you okay?"

She was crying so hard she couldn't talk. Byron, being terrified, because he had never seen her this way didn't know what to do. He pulled her into his lap and began rocking her back and forth while running his fingers in her hair. In a few minutes time she spoke. Just one sentence.

"I-I think I have to pee."

She got up slowly and climbed out of bed still crying, she thought she knew what was happening, but she wasn't certain. She didn't want to think about what was happening inside of her body. She was terrified.

Byron knew what was happening as soon as she got out of bed. There was a large blood stain right where she had been lying. He started tearing up as soon as he saw the proof; he knew Ruby had just had a miscarriage. When he heard Ruby crying in the bathroom even louder than before he jumped up to go and hold her. She knew she just had a miscarriage. When he got in the bathroom he almost choked on his tears, Ruby looked so sad and defeated.

She was lying on the floor in front of the toilet all curled up in the fetal position. She was holding her stomach. She wasn't ready to let that baby go. The sight of Ruby looking like this really got to him, and he was tearing up even more than before. He thought, they hadn't even seen the baby, not even on an ultrasound, how could they love something so much. That baby didn't even really exist yet. He made himself sit down next to Ruby and he kissed her forehead and started rubbing her back. When she felt him trying to comfort her, she tried to sit up, she wanted to lean up against him, but he told her to hold still, he would come down to her level.

"What . . . did . . . I . . . do . . . wrong, . . . Byron? I know I'm new to this, but I thought I did everything right."

"Love, there was nothing you could have done differently. We need to call Dr. Toroya, he'll probably want to see you. I'll go get the phone and call him. Please don't move, I'll be right back."

Ruby looked at Byron with her eyes filled with tears and gave him a sad, "Okay."

Byron reached Dr. Toroya and told him what happened during their sexual activity earlier in the day that may have caused this. Dr. Toroya told him there was no way that could have happened. Dr. Toroya asked Byron what was going on tomorrow and Byron told him that he and Ruby were getting married tomorrow afternoon. Dr. Toroya told Byron that Ruby needed to be under constant watch and that meant he could come to the wedding or she would have to come to the hospital for the next couple of days. Byron told the doctor that there was no way in hell he was calling off the wedding. He refused to. He would not allow anyone to take away one more thing that she really wanted. So instead of ruining the wedding for Ruby he invited Dr. Toroya to attend the wedding.

"Dr. Toroya will be coming to the wedding tomorrow so you don't have to go to the hospital. Are you okay? Can I do anything to help you? Do you want some Tylenol?"

"Thank you for not taking me to the hospital, I'm really glad the wedding is still on. I-I was afraid you wouldn't want to marry me anymore when you saw what just happened. God, I feel like such a damn defect. Like I'm broken and need to be turned in for parts, I feel like I just shattered your dreams for our family."

She started crying again and was so upset that she was gasping for breath and said, "I still want you, all of you, and I need you. Come here and hold me please."

"Honey, with what you just went through, I couldn't help but still want you. You were carrying our baby, but we both know it didn't even have a heartbeat yet so really it's like you had a rough period. I want you to think about it like that. We didn't loose a child, you just had a heavy period. Okay. Do it for me. Please? Now I am going to help you get cleaned up. You're body has been put through enough for one night."

Byron put the phone back on the cradle, then he scooped her up and helped her out of her robe. He started pulling his clothes off and picked her up again and then they got in the shower and he sat her down on the wall seat. He washed and conditioned her hair, then he lathered up her sponge and started washing her body. He started with her legs, arms, then her upper body. He was avoiding her southern most region and she knew it.

"Babe, I don't hurt down there. You can clean me up or you can give me the sponge and I'll do it myself."

"That's okay, I'll do it, I just didn't want to hurt you."

With a feather-light touch he wiped at her crotch and bottom. He saw her quiver and it scared him.

"What? What did I do? Did I hurt you?"

"No. Nothing like that. It just tickled a little bit."

Byron looked at her with mock astonishment.

"Are you ready for bed yet, babe? With what you just went through tonight you need to sleep, I don't know how you couldn't be tired."

"I need to find a pair of panties, a pad, and the Tylenol you asked me about earlier. It seems as though I can't go completely commando tonight. Sorry."

"Don't be sorry for me, especially not now. I'll take care of you. Where can I find all that stuff?"

"Well my panties are in the back of my second drawer, the pads are under my sink, in the back of the cabinet, and the Tylenol is in the medicine cabinet."

Byron got out of the shower and dried off, then went on his scavenger hunt. When he came back she had turned off the water and was fixing to get out. Byron stopped her.

"What are you doing?"

"I was going to get a towel and dry off."

"No, you're not. I'll get it for you, now sit back down. I said I'd take care of you, and I mean it. Here put your panties on like a big girl and take your medicine, and stop trying to do stuff. Let me take care of you. This is a tough thing to go through and I wish you could realize that. It is a body changing ordeal, and you really should stop and take it easy."

She stood up anyway and got right in front of her sexy beast and kissed him hard and said, "Honey, I've never been a princess, I'm a mechanic and I'm tougher than I look. Really, I'm okay. My legs don't hurt. Even if I was in a little bit of pain, I have a high tolerance for it."

"Ruby, why do you think I fell in love with you? Now I also see that you can be stubborn too, and I like a challenge."

Byron leaned down and kissed her, picked her up and carried her to the chair by the bed in their room while he went to go find clean sheets for the bed. He came back and changed them very quickly, then he picked her up off of the chair and tucked her into bed on her side. He gathered up the dirty sheets and went down stairs and tossed them in the washer. By the time he got back upstairs Ruby was already asleep. He got into bed quietly trying not to nudge or move her, or the bed. Ruby felt Byron getting into bed. She rolled toward him and laid her head on his chest and was humming in her sleep. He thought she looked at peace.

Finally, he thought, maybe now she can rest.

Chapter 16

"Ahhh!" Ruby woke up and stretched. She felt better this morning than she did last night and she was happy about that. She opened her eyes and saw Byron staring at her.

"What?"

"How do you feel? Are you in any pain?"

"I'm fine, really. A little sore, but like you said, I can easily associate that to a heavy period. You were right about that. It does help me by thinking it was a period. I made myself forget that I was even pregnant."

"I'm glad I could help in some way. I felt so useless, I'm really glad you couldn't see yourself. You really looked like someone was taking away your soul. I don't want you to forget about the almost baby, but I also don't want you to dwell on it. It bothered me seeing you like that last night. By the way, Dr. Toroya is going to be here soon, so maybe you should get dressed."

Byron asked her what she wanted to wear and when she started to get up he said, "Sit your sexy little ass back down! Dr. Toroya said you were supposed to take it very easy damn it, and that's what you are going to do."

"Okay, fine. Sorry, I forgot. Honey, will you please grab my sweats for me and some kind of shirt with buttons for when I go and get my hair done."

"That's better. Absolutely honey, I would love nothing more than to get that stuff for you."

He came back to the bed with her sweats, one of his button down shirts, and a thick pair of socks. He helped her get dressed then said, "About your appointment."

"Oh, no, what, Lilly can't do it can she?"

"Calm down babe, breathe."

"I'm breathing."

"Your hair and makeup person is coming here to get you ready instead of you having to be taken all over town."

"How did you manage to get her to come way out here?"

"Connections sweetheart, remember? Also, Cindy went to get both of your dresses and flowers."

"Wow, so I have absolutely nothing at all to do today."

"Not a thing. You get to be gorgeous. Check. You get to be loved on. Check. I get to marry you today and be the happiest man in the world. Check."

"Wow babe, that's some list. Before everyone starts getting here I want to talk to you." "Okay babe, shoot."

"How happy were you when we found out we were pregnant?"

"I was extremely happy. It was like you were giving me a gift that I in no way wanted to return."

"Really, you were that happy? I was happy, too. I was already starting to dream of what she would look like. I had a dream and she was about three. She had dark auburn hair with large curls and sapphire blue eyes, just like ours. Byron she was gorgeous. I want her."

Tears were welling up in her eyes and she said, "Byron I want a baby. I want to be pregnant again."

"Dr. Toroya says it could take a couple of weeks to get pregnant, but, he didn't say anything about practicing, and if you're feeling up to it then I'll be gentle."

"Oh, really, I like practice, and I really like it when you are gentle."

He leaned down and kissed her gently then pulled her up against him and then the doorbell rang.

"Damn it!" Byron said as he stomped down the stairs to the front door in his underwear and yanked it open.

"Oh, Dr. Toroya, please come in and excuse me, I'll be right back."

Byron ran back upstairs to the bedroom, looked at Ruby and said, "Dr. Toroya's here, and why didn't you tell me I was still in my underwear?"

"I like you in your underwear." She yelled into the closet. Then Byron came out wearing jeans that were zipped, but not buttoned. He scooped her up off the bed and carried her downstairs to the living room, and set her down on the couch next to Dr. Toroya.

"Ruby, how do you feel? Any pressure? Any discomfort?" Dr. Toroya asked her.

"I feel fine. Really. Please don't fuss over me, I'll get a complex."

"Honey, every now and then I am going to fuss over you. You need to know that. So you also need to learn to deal with it."

Byron told Dr. Toroya about everyone coming here to keep Ruby still today. Then Dr. Toroya made a strange suggestion. He said, "Ruby maybe someone could put a chair at the end of the alter and you could sit down during the ceremony."

"ABSOLUTELY NOT! I will not sit down. I will walk up the short aisle and stand during the ceremony just like every other bride before me has done. Honey, I'm sorry, but that is where I draw the line. No one in my family or yours even knew we were pregnant and now that we aren't anymore, I really don't intend to tell them. Cindy is the only one that knows what happened and it's going to stay that way. I'm going to be fine. I'm getting married today while I stand at the end of that aisle. I don't want to be treated any differently than normal."

Not another word was said about her walking up the aisle, so, she figured she won that argument. And since she won that argument she decided she'd let Byron carry her around all day if it made him feel better. She would rather he didn't want to carry her around, but she wouldn't fight it. She loved how much he wanted to take care of her, and being that close to him didn't make her feel bad either.

A knock on the front door told her that Cindy was here. Her best friend ran into the house carrying two white garment bags and Scott was right behind her carrying a cardboard box containing both of their bouquets. Cindy laid the garment bags on the back of the chair and ran to hug her best friend.

"Ruby, are you okay?

Ruby knew she would be concerned even more in person than she was on the phone. But Ruby felt totally aware of her feelings. They both knew she just had a miscarriage and even though Ruby should be upset she seemed okay.

"Cindy, not you, too. I'm fine, really. I want to get through this day so I can be alone with my husband. Practicing."

Byron looked at Ruby and gave her a grin. Ruby smiled back at him then she blushed. He knew exactly what she was thinking about. He was unsure if they should be practicing so soon, but he wouldn't disappoint Ruby.

Two hours later Ruby was still on the couch, but she had eaten, been carried to the bathroom twice, and had her hair and makeup done. Byron did his best not to gawk at her even though in his eyes she was the most gorgeous and sensuous woman he had ever laid his eyes on, and he loved telling her that fact of her life.

When it came time for Ruby to put on her dress she had Byron and Cindy's help. Cindy held the dress up and open while Byron placed her down inside of it; he sat her on the edge of the bed and then walked out of the room and closed the door. He didn't want to break tradition, but he didn't trust Ruby with lifting her . . . . anything, and he was the strongest man to get the job done, except for Scott. But, there was no way he would let Scott see his woman half naked. Not a chance.

Cindy pulled the satin laces tight enough that she could still breathe and made a bow at the bottom of her corset topped dress. She had to stand up, she wanted to see herself completely done up in the mirror. Cindy started to protest, but Ruby gave her a look that almost always gave her what she wanted.

"Ruby, I swear if you hurt yourself I'm telling Byron."

"Yeah, yeah, I know, relax. I'm fine. I'm not even bleeding anymore."

"That was quick. I thought you would bleed for at least a few days."

"Me, too. Oh, well. I'm not going to complain about it."

Ruby stood in front of the mirror and finally gave herself her full attention. She saw herself looking completely happy. She looked beautiful. She knew that Byron would think she was beautiful, too. She couldn't wait to see him in his tux. She was very curious to see what the guys were going to be wearing. She knew he would be handsome in whatever he chose to wear. He was always handsome. Soon he would be just hers and she couldn't wait to belong to only him. To be Mr. and Mrs. Miller.

The wedding was going to start at three and the guests were starting to arrive at two. She was happy they decided to have the ceremony and the reception at their house. Ruby's mother, father, and step-father all arrived on time, even though they all rode separately. That had to count for something. Her youngest sister Jami was the first sibling to arrive; she drove Ruby's step-father, Larry. Larry and Ruby's mom divorced a few years after they had Ruby's half-sister Jami, but Ruby thought of her half sister without the half. They were sisters, completely, no matter what anyone had to say. Plus, Larry had been in Ruby's life so long and taught her everything that she knew about vehicles and working with her hands, that there was no way she was going to cut him out of her life like some other family members seem to have done. The story of her mom and dad went back to when they were in high school, they were in love, got married sometime after her mom graduated, and then when her mom was twenty, Ruby was born. Ten years later they divorced. But not before giving Ruby two more sisters, Rebecca and Heather. It was very rough being young and going through two divorces, but she was strong and felt certain that that had helped her become how strong she was today. She didn't know if her sister Rebecca was coming out. She had been in California recently and Ruby wasn't sure if she would be able to afford the trip or not. Heather and her husband Thomas were stationed in a different part of California, and the last Ruby heard was that they were coming home. The family was going to be all together again, heaven help us all.

Chapter 17

Ruby stood in front of the mirror in her bedroom holding her flowers while her family crowded around her snapping pictures, and hugging each other excessively. Ruby's dad came into her bedroom with red eyes and said, "Hey big girl, you're not gonna cry are you?"

"Nope, I'm good. Dad, please don't cry. I love him and there is no reason to cry. You know what, could you guys give me a second, I need some privacy."

"You okay?" Cindy asked.

"Absolutely, but here, could you take this box to Byron and tell him it's his wedding gift from me. And tell him, I love him."

"Will do."

Then Cindy turned and was gone. Ruby had finished working on that '55 Chevy truck and had Scott bring it out to the house today. The box she sent Cindy away with held the only key that would start up that old truck. Byron had told her he liked the truck after they left the shop on the day they made love in it, and he also liked the way she had to lean down and under the hood to work on it.

A few minutes before the ceremony was supposed to start there was a knock on the door, and then Byron came through the doors with his eyes closed then turned around shut the door and turned back around and put his arms out. He said, "Ruby, come here to me, please, I won't look at you, I want to kiss you. How did you know I wanted the truck?"

Ruby stepped away from the mirror toward Byron and grabbed his hands. He immediately pulled her to him then reached a hand to her face to find her lips, and he planted a deep long kiss right on *his* Ruby. When he broke the kiss he told her to lead him to the bed. When she had him at the bed he told her to sit down, and he sat down right beside her.

"I saw you eyeing the truck while I was working on it, and you said you liked it while you made love to me in it. Don't you remember? It was just a project truck. I was going to fix it then turn around and sell it. When I saw how much you wanted it, I just couldn't part with it."

"I remember the way you were laid out in it. Everything else is kind of a blur. Thank you sweetheart, I love the truck, and I love you and here you go. These are for you."

While he still had his eyes closed, he reached into his jacket pocket and pulled out a box and an envelope. Then he asked, "Which one do you want to open first?"

"The box, I guess."

He handed her the long, black, velvet box and she opened it slowly and saw a beautiful string of pearls.

"Honey, oh my, these are beautiful."

"Well, I know you don't have any and every grown woman should own at least one pearl. So now you have a whole string of them. Here, now open this one."

He held out the envelope and she grabbed it and tore it open. She gasped and he opened his eyes, afraid she might be choking or something. She took a few minutes to look at the papers.

"You want to rebuild my shop out here, near the house?"

The envelope he handed her held blueprints and a contract with one of the building companies in this area.

"Yep, that way you're always close to home."

"Aw, babe, thank you. God, I love you, have I told you that lately?"

"I love you, too, now can we go and get married?" He closed his eyes again.

"Let's go. I've been waiting for this since I met you, Byron."

He walked out the door first and headed downstairs and to the back door and outside to where the ceremony would be held. Her dad was standing in the doorway holding her flowers and she asked him if he would help her with her pearls.

"Byron gave them to me. Do you like them?"

"Yes, they're beautiful, just like you. He is a very lucky man."

He took the pearls from her hand and fastened the clasp around the back of her neck. Her dad grabbed her arm and led her down the stairs toward the back door. Larry was at the bottom of the stairs waiting to hug Ruby. When he embraced her, Ruby cried for a second. She loved her dysfunctional family. There was some stability in it, but it normally came from her. She was always the neutral ground that brought the family together. He whispered he loved her and she told him thank you and that she loved him, too. Ruby let go of her step-father and headed to the back door while she wiped at the tears under her eyes. Cindy was at the door already holding her flowers and when she saw Ruby coming she said, "Oh my god, look at you. You look like someone completely different."

"Thanks, I think."

Dr. Toroya came up to Ruby and whispered into her ear.

"You look gorgeous, but do you feel okay?"

Instead of talking she just nodded her head and smiled at him. He hugged her neck and went outside to find a seat underneath the large white tent.

The wedding music started and Cindy looked back at Ruby then turned and walked out to her march. Ruby looked at her dad and smiled, then he bent her arm around his elbow and when they heard the wedding march she started walking, towing her dad behind her. She was so excited and it showed on her face. The first thing she saw was his face. He was wide eyed and smiling at her, she loved to see him smile. She noticed that Scott was in a typical black tux and her sexy beast was wearing a white tux. Apparently he was still trying to convince everyone that they had abstained. When they got to the end of the aisle, her dad faced her, kissed her on the cheek, and then placed her hand in Byron's hand. At that point, she knew she was home. She knew she found the perfect man for her.

The ceremony progressed, Byron and Ruby said their I do's proudly and when the preacher said, "Mr. Miller you may now kiss your bride." Ruby blushed at him. Byron scooped Ruby up off of the ground and cradled her in his arms. He leaned down to her and kissed her long and hard. When everyone started clapping she remembered where she was at the same time Byron was pulling away from the kiss.

Slowly he turned and carried Ruby back to the house. The music started again and people were rising from their chairs to give hugs and their congratulations. Ruby and Byron met everyone at the door and received their hugs fairly quickly, they were happy at that point that they had a small ceremony. As soon as the hugs stopped Byron turned to face Ruby and said, "Mrs. Miller, you look so beautiful. Would you mind dancing with me?" Ruby took Byron's hand and said, "Mr. Miller I would love to dance with you." They made it into the back yard where the D.J. was set up and they danced. They kissed through most of the dance, but neither of them minded all the on-lookers. Ruby's dad tapped Byron on the shoulder and asked, "Byron, do you mind if I cut in?"

"Not as long as I get her back." Byron said as he smiled at her dad then gave her a peck on the lips. Ruby's dad was tearing up while he was dancing with her. She kept telling him it was okay. He kept saying stuff like, I can't believe my big girl is a married woman now.

At almost the end of the song Byron walked up to Ruby's dad and tapped his shoulder and said, "Okay sir, times up. I need my Ruby back."

"I was wondering when you would come back and claim her. Please, call me dad."

"Okay, dad, I really need Ruby. Scott is fixing to give the toast. Come on, love."

Ruby reached her hand out to Byron and he grabbed it in his hand and pulled her close. Very sneakily he took a step behind her and scooped her up into his arms again and carried her to where the cake was.

"I figured you'd pick me up, again. Especially since you could see how well I did during the ceremony."

"You're doing fine. Dr. Toroya said so. I just want to hold you close."

"Please, Mr. Miller, don't let me stop you. I'll let you hold me as close as you can possibly get me. And when did Dr. Toroya tell you that I was doing okay?"

"When you were dancing with your dad. I told him to tell me if you seemed off, in any way so I could be your sexy beast and carry you all around this place."

"Byron, you can't do that."

"Oh, yeah, and who's going to stop me?"

"I didn't mean that you can't, I mean you shouldn't, because if you start doing that then I may want you to carry me everywhere."

"I think I can do that, babe. You are as light as a feather, it's not like you'd help me throw my back out."

"Ha Ha Ha."

They got to the table where the cake was set up and there were already two glasses with champagne in them. Scott handed them their glasses and began his toast. It didn't last to long, but that was okay with them. When he finished his speech, Ruby and Byron crossed arms and sipped out of their glasses. Then set them down and kissed, again. Ruby's mom interrupted their kiss and said, "Time to cut your cake."

"Mom, really, right now? Can't you see I'm marking my territory?"

"I don't think anyone would mess with me while you are around. Do you remember that guy at the bar, and what you did to his nose?"

"Oh, yeah."

Byron set Ruby on her feet and stood behind her while her mother situated them for a photo opportunity with the cake knife in their joined hands.

"Byron, would you like to eat your cake or wear your cake?"

"I don't care, but you'll be wearing yours so I can lick it off of you when I kiss you."

Ruby blushed and then gave Byron her little grin and he knew he would be getting his cake smeared all over his face, too. Just as promised Ruby took a piece of cake for Byron and got just a little bit on the outside corner of his mouth. Then when he swallowed his piece of cake, she leaned in and sucked the cake off his lip and then kissed his lip in the same spot. He gazed at her hungrily. It was her turn. Byron got a smaller piece of cake from Ruby's mother and held it up to Ruby's mouth. She opened her mouth for him and he rubbed the cake all over her lips then pushed it in her mouth on top of her tongue. Then if front of both of their families he completely covered her mouth with his and sucked lightly, getting all of the cake off her face then kissed her deeply. When she opened her eyes after that kiss, her eyes were half closed and she had that devilish grin in place. Yep, mission accomplished, Ruby was ready and tonight she would get what she wanted. Ruby said, "Byron, I think I should go and throw the bouquet now."

Ruby let go of Byron's hand and called all the single women to the center of the dance area. When they were all in place, Ruby turned her back to the girls and tossed the bouquet in the air. Jami jumped up high and came down with the bouquet in her hands. Ruby turned to Byron and said, "Now, it's your turn. You get to throw my garter."

"Okay, hang on let me get you a chair. Hey single guys only, it's time. Come on, gather around."

When Byron had the chair in place he picked Ruby up and sat her down in the chair. He got down on one knee, stuck his hand up her dress, and kissed her while his hand went higher than her garter and he caressed her inner thigh. Very slowly he stuck his other hand up her dress and began working the garter down her leg. He pulled back from the kiss and looked at her face, she had her eyes half closed and he knew he was still turning her on. He pulled her garter off the rest of the way and shot it into the crowd of men. Byron's cousin Jeremy caught it and put it on his head like a headband. Watching Jeremy run around with her garter that close to his face made Ruby blush scarlet, something Byron didn't think was possible. Byron had never seen her blush like this before.

"Ruby that is a beautiful blush. What are you thinking about?"

"Well, your cousin, and the fact that he is wearing my garter around his head after it was around my thigh. And the fact that I know what I want to do to you tonight."

"Really, you have my attention. What do you want to do to me tonight?"

"Come here and I'll tell you."

Ruby got right up to Byron's ear and whispered everything that she wanted to do to him. Byron responded by calling attention to the reception party and telling everyone that the party was over, because he would love to take his wife away on their honeymoon. Hugs and kisses were given out again and then the crowd dispersed. It was going to be one hell of a honeymoon.

Chapter 18

Packing for their honeymoon was easy enough; Byron dumped all the contents from her naughty drawer into a duffel bag while she packed two weeks worth of clothes. Then Byron was packing his clothes in his bag while Ruby was downstairs in the kitchen packing up some munchies for the road. He loved looking at her in her dress, and asked her not to change, yet. They were going to the house on the island for their honeymoon. When Byron was finished packing he grabbed all the bags from upstairs and headed down to the kitchen. He dropped the bags at the back door and scooped up his new wife right into his arms and asked, "Are you ready to go, Mrs. Miller? The chariot you rebuilt awaits us."

"You really want to drive your, old-new truck, already. I am so glad you like it."

"Love, that's our truck. Now let's get going, I'm ready for some practice and for what you said you wanted to do to me."

Ruby kissed his mouth before he could put another thought together, then let go just as fast. He set her down and went to take the bags and the box out to the truck. When the truck was loaded he went inside, picked up his beautiful wife and carried her out to the truck and put her in the passenger seat. He ran back to the house one last time and locked up.

The ride to the beach house was no longer than the last trip, but still tiring. He wanted her to rest the whole way, but all she wanted to do was kiss him the whole way, and she did. Every time they stopped, she would lean over and kiss him hard, then he would get rock hard and threaten to rip her dress off right there at that red light. When they finally got to the house Byron went around to her door, opened it then carried her up the back steps to the house, he managed to unlock the house with one hand while he held her. Then he pushed open the door and carried her over the threshold. He sat her down in the recliner, where he proposed to her about two weeks ago and ran back to the truck to get the bags and the box. With every thing in his hands he kicked the door shut and locked it. Then he dropped the bags and walked over to her holding the sex swing and said, "I think it is time we start practicing."

"I can't wait."

When they woke up the next morning, all sprawled out on top of the covers and covered in chocolate sauce, Ruby couldn't help but giggle. Her giggle woke Byron up and he looked at her with a grin.

"Mr. Miller, what are you thinking about right now?"

"I am thinking about taking you into the shower and having you for dessert. Again. I had a lot of fun last night. I swear I didn't know you could bend like that."

"Well, babe, we definitely need a shower, and I could use some dessert, too."

They both got out of bed and walked to the bathroom and got in the shower. They played more than they cleaned, but it was their honeymoon and they could if they wanted, too.

Plus, there was no family around to discourage them. When they did get completely clean, they got out and got dressed. Byron told Ruby he wanted to take her into town so he could show off his new wife. The plan was to go and see a movie and then go and eat lunch. Ruby told Byron she wanted to have him all to herself for the next two week. They got in the truck she built for him and headed to the large theater in the middle of town. They got inside the theater and went to the candy stand. They got their drinks and showed the man at the ticket booth that they were going to see the comedy and he let them pass. They laughed through the whole movie. Byron was thinking that he had never seen Ruby laugh this much. He liked it. She had the sweetest laugh. One part in the movie was so funny it had her in tears from laughing so hard. He couldn't help but join in on her laughter.

"Ruby, I'm glad you like this movie. I like seeing you laugh like this."

"Like what?"

"Like you don't care if someone sees you crying from laughing so hard. I know how aware of yourself you are."

"I think it has something to do with being around you so much. I'm really comfortable."

"Babe, it shows."

He leaned over and kissed her lightly on her lips. She accepted his kiss lovingly and said, "Mr. Miller, that was really gentle. When do I get more of that gentleness?"

"As soon as we get home. Let's plan on that being later tonight."

"Then you had better stop teasing me like that. If you don't then I may not want to wait for tonight."

An evil grin crossed his face, but he did his best to hide it before she noticed. He really was still worried about her. She didn't need to have this much activity. Especially since what they deemed as "the incident" just happened two days ago. He wanted to have her, but he didn't want it to be impossible for them to get pregnant by hurting her in some way.

When the movie ended Ruby had dark streaks running down her face from her makeup and all the crying she did. Byron looked at her and said, "Hey Ruby, you look cute like this, but you may want to go to the bathroom and wipe your eyes."

"Oh, god. Do I look like a raccoon? I knew I should have worn waterproof mascara today."

"It's great. Let's go."

They made their way to the lobby and Ruby ran into the bathroom. When she got inside she couldn't help but laugh at herself. She looked ridiculous. She couldn't understand how Byron kept himself from laughing at her. She quickly cleaned up and headed back out to the lobby to meet her husband.

"That's better, babe. You look gorgeous again."

"How is it that you managed not to laugh at me?"

"I don't want to laugh at you. With you, definitely. But at you, no way. I didn't want to hurt your feelings. I know how self conscious you are."

"Stop treating me like a princess. There is a time and place for it. If I look funny laugh at me, otherwise I wouldn't know. Be honest with me and I'll be honest with you."

"I'll try to remember that, love."

They walked down the street and stopped at an outdoor restaurant and ate lunch under a large umbrella. When they finished eating Bryon told Ruby he had a surprise for her.

"What is it?"

"It's not an it, it's a place."

"I seem to remember a previous conversation going in this direction."

"It's not the prom or any kind of dance."

"Well, that narrows it down a little bit doesn't it."

Byron led Ruby to the corner of the street and held his thumb out. A passing horse carriage stopped and asked which way they were going. Byron said, "Sir, I would like to take my new bride to the pier."

"Not a problem sir, please Miss, climb on up."

Ruby and Byron climbed into the carriage and Ruby was thrilled.

"Byron I have never ridden in a horse drawn carriage before, either."

"I know that. Why do you think you are right now? I want to show you things that you have never experienced. Your life with me is going to be full of surprises. I promise you that."

"I like surprises, Byron. I want to see new things and do new things with you, too."

The carriage ride was amazing. The driver took them all over the water front before he took them to the pier. When the carriage got to the edge of the pier, Byron paid the man and then asked him if he could come back for them in a couple of hours. The man agreed and clucked to his horses. Ruby watched the white carriage with its two white horses disappear out of sight. Byron grabbed her hand and led her to the pier. His plan was to sit on one of the many benches and watch the dolphins in the water.

Ruby wrapped her arm around his back and stuck her hand in his back pocket. The pier was long with plenty of benches, but Byron didn't seem to want to choose one. He just kept walking, all the way to the end.

"Byron, are we going to stop soon? If not we arc going to run out of pier to walk on."

"I want to take you to the end. I want to be alone with you in public."

"That doesn't make much sense, but I get it."

"Ruby, how are you feeling? You haven't said anything about "the incident" since the morning of the wedding; I just want to make sure you are okay."

"I'm fine, I swear to you, I am having so much fun here. There is one thing that I want from you."

"Oh, yeah, what's that?"

"Well, I know what just happened to us isn't something that I should take lightly, but since I have already stopped bleeding there is no reason why I shouldn't be able to try to get pregnant. Byron I want you."

"Ruby, I love you, and I want you to be pregnant, too, but it's not up to us and you know that. But I promise you, I will do everything in my power to try to make that happen."

"I love you, Byron."

"Ruby, without you I wouldn't be as happy as I am. I love you, too."

Ruby and Byron sat at the end of the pier for the longest time. Two hours later they were at the entrance of the pier waiting for their carriage to pick them up. The carriage was prettier now that the sky was darkening. The white really glowed and the cloth top was pulled up to block the wind. Byron helped Ruby in and then he climbed in behind her. Ruby was leaned up against his side and his arm was around her shoulders, they were on a romantic carriage ride in town for everyone to see, and she didn't care. She was totally at ease. Byron had made her completely comfortable with herself.

Chapter 19

Ruby and Byron were down to the last full day of their honeymoon and they intended to spend that day completely wrapped up in each others arms. They stayed in bed all day and watched movies back to back. Taking an occasional break for eating, going to the bathroom, or sex. It was becoming a routine today. Ruby didn't mind, she knew what she and Byron wanted most out of this honeymoon. She was going to get pregnant or die from too much sex, which ever one came first.

Byron was a little ticked that the honeymoon went by so fast. He knew that when he got home he would still have Ruby all to himself, so he didn't act too upset. After the eighth movie that day, Ruby decided they were having breakfast for dinner. She jumped out of bed in only Byron's t-shirt and headed down to the kitchen. She was going to make scrambled eggs, grits, and sausage links. She pulled everything she would need out of the fridge and got to work. She loved making breakfast, it didn't matter what time of day it was.

"Hey there sexy, can I do anything to help?"

"You can set the table or we can eat in bed. It doesn't matter to me. Where do you want to eat?"

"How about lets sit right here on the counter."

"That's fine."

When everything was ready she divided it up on the fine china Byron had pulled out.

"These were my great-grandmothers dishes. Nobody has eaten off of these plates in like sixty years. My granny would have liked you."

"Didn't your other relatives want to use them when she passed?"

"No everyone was already married and had already picked out their own china patterns. Everything that wasn't needed came to this house. They have been sitting in that cabinet forever. I'm glad I get to use them with someone I love."

"Byron, you are too good to me, do you know that."

"Nothing's too good for you. I'm perfect to you and for you."

"Byron, you're going to make me cry. Please change the subject. I know. How is your breakfast?"

"Breakfast is great; I haven't had grits in years. I honestly wasn't aware that anyone still knew how to make it. Now, let's backpedal, how would I make you cry?"

"You know me. I don't do well with my emotions. If I'm not mad and punching somebody, then I'm laughing until I cry, or if I get too much love from you I'll cry, because I don't know how to express exactly how I feel about you. I love you so much that I can't put it into words without blubbering."

"I know you love me, you don't have to over exaggerate it."

"Byron, I'm not exaggerating."

Byron looked into her eyes and knew she was telling him the truth. She couldn't and wouldn't lie to him and he thought he should have kicked his own ass for even thinking it.

"I'm sorry, Ruby. I understand how you feel, because I feel that way, too."

Byron leaned over to Ruby on the counter and kissed her tenderly. She slowly pushed her plate aside so she could put herself on his lap facing him. She wanted to make-out completely with her new husband. Byron started the kiss with his hand on her back and when it became more intense he reached down with both hands and grabbed her bare ass and moaned deep in his throat. He had completely forgotten she was naked under his shirt. When he came to that realization he suddenly wanted to devour her. He became instantly erect underneath her. She noticed every inch of his arousal.

In a whisper Ruby said, "Byron, the bed is all the way upstairs. What are we going to do?"

Byron moved everything off of the kitchen island onto the nearby countertop and said, "We are going to be up here on the counter."

Bryon slid Ruby off of him then jumped to his feet on the floor. Byron dropped his boxers to his ankles and then kicked them off. Ruby was fixing to start taking off her shirt and Byron said, "Hold on. Let me take care of that." Byron grabbed the shirt at the collar and ripped it straight down the front, right off of her. He looked at Ruby and said, "Are you ready, or do you need my assistance ma'am?"

"I think I'm okay sir, how about you."

"I was born ready."

Byron climbed back onto the island and helped Ruby up to sit on his lap facing him. She perched herself on his member and they began rocking while they kissed each other. All Ruby could hear was Byron hissing under his breath. When Byron bit her where she liked it, he got to hear her squeal. Other than her squeal she was moaning loudly. He knew what power he possessed when it came to his wife.

"Ruby, you ready?"

"You know where to unload, honey."

Byron released a forceful load into her. Exactly where she wanted it. Their sex had been so great this time that she was trembling when he finished.

"Ruby, why are you shaking? Are you okay?"

"Babe, that was amazing. It was magical, without the white rabbit and the top hat. I think I'm coming off of a sexual high."

Ruby pulled herself off of Byron and slid over on the counter. Byron kissed her lightly and hopped down. "Ruby, I'm going to go take a shower. Do you want to join me?"

"No, you go ahead. I am going to clean up down here. Plus, we should get packing soon. I don't want to go home, but that's just too bad. We really need to go back to work tomorrow."

"I am going to go and take my shower now; when I get done I'll help you pack everything up."

"Hurry up, I miss you already."

Byron turned to see Ruby blowing him a kiss as he walked toward the staircase. All he could think about in his shower was the wonderful woman in the kitchen. She knew how to cook real southern food, she loved hanging out in a guys surroundings, she didn't care if she got dirty, and she had a mean right hook. She was everything he wanted. She had given herself to him completely before they got married, because she was ready to be with him, he didn't need to push or persuade her. He loved that she took some risks and he wanted to be there when she decided to take more risks.

Byron got out of the shower and pulled on a pair of jeans and just zipped them up, then headed down stairs. He was determined to keep her in a calm state of mind. When he got to the kitchen, he noticed it was already cleaned and the box of munchies they brought down was already packed up and sitting on the table, ready to go.

"Ruby, where are you?"

"In the dining room." she called.

Byron made his way to the dining room and found Ruby sitting on the floor in front of the china cabinet.

"What are you doing, love?"

"I was thinking, maybe we should take your granny's china to our house. Then we can use it more often."

"I think she'd like that. Hang on let me go and find a box."

Byron came back into the dining room with the box that the munchies were in. He also found some newspaper to wrap all the old dishes in. They didn't need to get broken on the trip. Ruby and Byron sat together in the dining room and wrapped up every dish in that cabinet. They were going to take the whole collection and the cabinet to their house. Ruby gave him the idea. But, he knew she was right. He wouldn't want to hide the beautiful dishes in his kitchen cabinets, he needed a china cabinet.

When the box was packed to capacity and taken into the kitchen, Byron and Ruby moved the cabinet to the back door so they could load it up in the morning. Hand in hand they walked through their beach house and locked up and turned off the lights. When they got upstairs they pulled out their bags and started packing their clothes.

"Ruby we can leave the swing here if you want."

"That's fine. It can be the other reason we have to come back here."

"I like that idea. Everything else is going home with us, though."

"Somehow, babe, I knew you would say that."

"That's because, you have become very perceptive of me lately."

"It's a skill that I'm acquiring. I like that I can read you. Though you do make it easy, you know."

"I like it that you can read me, too. What am I thinking about right now?"

"Well from your tone of voice, I would have to say, you want to get me into the swing."

"Ding, ding, ding. You are right on the money, baby. Now how am I going to go about making that happen?"

"Well as soon as we pack we will have the rest of the night to play."

Byron shot her a flashy grin and said, "Then why aren't you done packing yet."

They both packed their bags in record speed, leaving out just one outfit for tomorrow. Byron threw their bags by the bedroom door and then walked over to Ruby on the other side of the bed. He grabbed her hand and pulled her to him. He kissed her cheek then her jaw line before moving to her mouth. When her lips parted he delved his tongue inside her mouth and began stroking hers. His other hand started rubbing her back then went lower to her hips, and slowly descended to squeeze a firm butt cheek. Byron was loving the way he could be with her. He had just had her in the kitchen not even two hours ago and here he was with her again. He was insatiable. He lifted Ruby up and sat her down in the swing that they had hanging from their bedroom ceiling. The location for the swing had been his choice.

Byron slowly pulled away from the kiss and kissed his way down her jaw line and neck. He kissed her chest, the swell of her breasts, and then lower. He kissed her abdomen and each protruding hip bone, slowly working his way to her core. He was moving slowly on purpose. He wanted to drive her out of her mind. It was working.

All Ruby could think about when he was kissing her down her front was how much she didn't want him to stop. He was so sweet and gentle with her and she loved him for it. Byron came back up for air and to kiss her. She accepted the kiss and let him linger in her mouth. When he decided to end the kiss he went down to nibble at her breasts.

"Oww, babe, easy. That hurt."

Byron jumped at the thought that he just hurt her.

"What did I do?"

"You bit me too hard."

"Baby, I barely bit you. I did it how I always do it."

Byron reached his hands out to her breasts and held them then asked, "Does this hurt?"

"It's not totally unbearable, but it feels a little tender."

"Ruby, why don't you go and take a shower while I run up to the drug store. I'll be right back."

"Why are you going to the drug store?"

"I think I may have given you what you wanted after all."

Byron gave Ruby a wide smile and kissed her forehead, then ran into the closet for a shirt. He emerged from the closet and Ruby was still standing there with her mouth open and a tear in her eye. She really looked like she was in shock.

"Ruby we don't know, yet. Relax love, go and take a shower. I'll be back as soon as you get out."

Since she still wasn't moving-just staring into space—Byron walked her back to the bed and helped her lay down. He kissed her forehead again and started rubbing her face, trying to break her concentration.

"Ruby, snap out of it. Are you okay? I need you to talk to me. I am not going until you do."

"Byron, what if what happened last time happens this time, too?"

"We can't dwell on the negative. If we do, nothing positive will come from our lives. We can only hope for the best. Now then. Love, are you going to be okay for about ten minutes. I am going to the drug store to get you a pregnancy test and I will be right back."

"I'll be fine. I am going to sit right here. I don't want my mind to run away with me and make me pass out or something while I'm in the shower."

"That's actually a good idea. I love you, I'll be right back."

"I love you too."

Byron turned from the bedroom and ran downstairs and headed for the back door and then his truck. On his way to the store all he could think about was how quickly this happened. He wasn't expecting this and she really caught him off guard with it. He was suddenly very glad he had talked to Dr. Toroya about what to expect if Ruby were to ever get pregnant. The doctor told him to keep an eye out for tenderness, swelling, and nausea. Nausea was a big one.

When he got in the store he asked a small woman behind the counter where he could find the pregnancy tests she pointed the direction out to him and he took off to locate them. He was very surprised by how many there were. He expected maybe two brands. There were at least ten. He did all he knew he could do. He grabbed three different tests and headed back to the counter. He paid the woman and grabbed the plastic bag and headed out to his truck. He wanted to get back to Ruby. He hated that he had to leave her alone, although he didn't want to drag her out of the house either. He finally decided his decision was justified. He pulled into his parking spot and jumped out of his truck and made a dead sprint for the back door. He plunged the key into the door handle and made his way inside. He slammed the door behind him and locked it back then ran up the stairs to the bedroom.

Ruby wasn't where he left her. He thought about panicking, then he heard the shower water running. He walked into the bathroom and saw Ruby sitting on the bench in the shower holding her stomach with her head down.

"Ruby, love, are you okay?"

Ruby picked her head up when she heard his voice and smiled in his direction.

"I feel fine. Did you get the test?"

"I actually got you three tests because there were so many to choose from. We are going to use them all."

Ruby jumped out of the shower and wrapped herself in a towel and reached out for the bag he was holding. Byron handed it over to her willingly. She set the bag on the counter and started pulling out the three boxes. She looked at Byron and smiled again. She picked one box up and started tearing it open. Byron was excited all of a sudden so he grabbed a box and started tearing it open, too. She let Byron open the last box while she went and peed in a cup that came in one of the boxes. When she was finished Byron said, "Okay we have to dip that one in the cup. The other two get two drops in the center of the stick. When we get that part done it says I have to hold you and kiss you for exactly five minutes maybe longer."

"Well since your kisses seem to make me more comfortable with everything I think I would like that."

They dipped the one test and closed it, then Ruby took the little dropper and placed two drops of her urine right in the center of the other two tests. When she finished she flushed the rest of the urine and tossed out all the trash. Byron reached around her and grabbed her stomach from behind. She spun around in his arms and kissed him. They were so in love, but five minutes was five minutes. At the five minute mark Ruby took a few steps back and sat on the toilet and Byron walked over to the counter and looked at the tests. He had to make sure he read the directions right, he didn't want to tell her the wrong news. Byron turned to Ruby then walked over to her. He knelt down in front of her and hugged her close to him and had to whisper to fight back the tears coming to his eyes.

"Ruby, you're pregnant. We're going to have a baby."

Chapter 20

9 months later

"Byron wake up. I think my water just broke."

Byron peeked his head up out of his pillow and with sleepy eyes looked at Ruby and said, "No honey, it's okay, I don't think those plastic water bottles actually break."

"No, Byron! Wake up! Look at me! My water just broke. Don't you feel the wetness in the bed?"

Sitting up quickly it hits him. "Oh, god, I have to get you to the hospital, right now."

"Yeah, good wake up. I don't hurt yet. Don't panic, please. Just minor contractions."

"I'm not panicking, I'm not panicking, what do I need to do?"

"Go make a pot of coffee, you need to wake up and I need the caffeine."

"Byron jumped out of bed and literally ran downstairs. He ran so fast that you would have thought someone had lit a fire under his ass. When he was running back upstairs, he ran into the bathroom to go pee, and then he brushed his teeth. Good to know someone was keeping up with his morning habits.

"Byron, my contractions are like fifteen minutes apart. When they get to be around seven minutes apart you have to take me to the hospital."

"Okay, I can remember that. Just tell me when they change intervals."

Byron was dressed two seconds after he got out of the bathroom. He slowly helped Ruby out of bed and then helped her out of her wet clothes. He went into the closet and pulled out one of his large t-shirts and a pair of large boxers. He set her in the chair and started pulling the wet sheets off the bed. Then an intense contraction hit her.

"AHH, OH MY GOD!"

Ruby screamed so loud that she actually made Byron jump.

"Ruby, breathe, okay. Just breathe."

"Byron, I am breathing, this really, hurts. I can yell if I want too."

"You're right, I'm sorry."

"Babe, please go and grab my shoes and sweat pants. Hurry, please."

Byron ran out of the bed room and into their closet to retrieve Ruby's sweat pants and the shoes that she already laid out. How has it already been nine months? He couldn't wrap his head around it. Time had passed so quickly. He ran back to Ruby and helped her get dressed and then he got down on the floor and put on her shoes and tied them for her. She had gotten so big, that she couldn't bend down for risk of hurting the baby.

"Byron, will you take our bags to the truck, please. I'll wait for you. I don't trust myself on the stairs."

"Yeah, but really, don't move a muscle. You aren't having a contraction right now are you?"

"No, that's why I want you to hurry."

"Be right back."

Byron turned for the stairs and disappeared. She heard him slam the truck door, so at least she knew he made it outside. She felt awful. She had been so moody for the last three months, and Byron being the nice guy seemed to understand that it was hormones, and let her yell at him. If the roles were switched she couldn't be sure that she wouldn't have bitched him out. They had gotten back from their honeymoon and knew they were pregnant. As soon as they got to the house and unloaded everything they went straight to Dr. Toroya's office. He called her a miracle patient and she smiled at him. He wanted to check her out for himself, and sure enough she was expecting, but what they hadn't know at the wedding was they were still pregnant. She hadn't actually had a miscarriage; it was just some blood loss. Ruby and Byron just laughed at each other when they heard that and they remembered their honeymoon when all they did was have sex around the clock. Dr. Toroya set her up with prenatal vitamins, and gave her a bunch of literature for her and Byron to read. Her concentration was broken by a contraction.

"B-Y-R-O-N!"

Ruby didn't have anything to hold on to, so she stood up and leaned up against the wall, facing it. When Byron heard her yell he became terrified again. He ran upstairs to see Ruby standing against the wall holding her stomach.

"You okay?"

"It was a contraction, but that one really hurt. Are we ready, yet?"

"I was putting coffee in the thermoses. Come on you can come down stairs with me this time, that way you can squeeze my hand, or yell at me."

Byron got right beside her and helped her walk to the bedroom door. When they got to the threshold she was already having another contraction. Byron felt helpless like before, he didn't like seeing her go through this pain. She was still standing and she squeezed her eyes shut tight and was almost bent over holding her belly. It sounded to him like she was whimpering. That did it. He waited until the contraction passed then he scooped her up into his arms and carried her out to the truck. He laid the seat back with her in it and told her to hang on. He ran back into the house and grabbed the coffee, the keys, and the cell phone. They were going to the hospital. He pulled the door shut and locked it behind him, then ran to his truck. When he got in Ruby still had her eyes closed and she was rubbing her stomach in one spot. He figured the baby was kicking her harder than usual. They told Dr. Toroya they didn't want to know the sex. Hell, they didn't even want a full ultrasound. Dr. Toroya used a hand held heart monitor. It had a small probe like the ultrasound machine but instead of seeing you could hear. They got to hear the heartbeat and they knew it was a strong baby, because the heart beat was fast and loud.

The hospital was about thirty minutes from their house, but thanks to Byron's connections, he got a police escort. The were in front of the hospital in ten minutes. Ruby had two contractions on the way and she screamed and squeezed Byron's hand through both of them. When he got out of the truck, Ruby was opening her door. He ran to her door and said, "I know good and damn well, you weren't fixing to jump out of this truck."

Ruby started crying and said, "No, I need you to carry me, I can't fell my legs anymore."

"What? Like at all?"

"I can't feel them. I feel the contractions, they are even more intense than before, but I can't feel my legs. Byron, I'm scared. What's happening?"

"I don't know, but we're fixing to find out."

Byron scooped Ruby up out of the truck and shut his truck door with his elbow. He tried to be careful with Ruby in his arms, but he wanted to run with her. He was really scared for her. When they got inside the ER the nurse behind the counter asked what the problem was and Byron told her that Ruby said she couldn't feel her legs. The woman actually pulled out paperwork and started asking questions.

"Look lady, I will come back out here and sign papers after I see Dr. Toroya and someone checks my wife. Something is wrong. The paperwork can wait."

The woman asked if he had insurance. That was all it took. Byron went to the emergency door and pushed his way through as the woman was yelling, "Sir you can't go through there."

"Oh yeah, watch me. Does anyone know where Dr. Toroya is? This is an emergency."

One doctor popped his head out of an exam room and said he was out of town. Ruby was having another contraction and she screamed again. The doctor came out of the other room and asked what was going on, how far apart her contractions were, and if anything else was wrong.

Ruby couldn't stand it anymore, she yelled, "I can't feel my damn legs, would you mind helping us out here. I would like to have this baby already."

Byron stood there speechless. He couldn't believe she just yelled at a complete stranger. The doctor told one of the orderly's to bring out a gurney, when it was in the hall Byron walked over to it and laid Ruby down. She wouldn't let go of his hand though. She refused to be separated from him. The doctor, the orderly, and two other nurses pushed her bed to a private room with Byron walking right beside her. Ruby looked at Byron and said, "I love you, and this hurts like hell. I think I know why your mom may have stopped at one."

"I swear to you, I will never put you through this again. I don't like seeing you in pain, I wish I could shield you from it, but there's nothing I can do."

"Yeah, there is. You can hold my hand and tell me you love me. You didn't do this to me by yourself. I wanted it, too."

The doctor busted back into the room and said, "Dr. Toroya is on his way, he had been out of town, but only thirty minutes out of town. Dr. Toroya said he didn't want to miss you giving birth." That put a slight smile on Ruby's face. Then the doctor was trying to make small talk.

"So do you know what you are having yet?"

Byron answered his questions, just incase Ruby had another contraction.

"No, we wanted to be surprised."

"Okay, do you know how many you're having?"

That question made Ruby and Byron stop and stare at each other then they looked at the doctor.

Byron asked, "Doc. Do you know something we should know?"

"Well, it is my medical opinion that since she is so big, it is probably twins. What did you weigh before you got pregnant?"

"About ninety five pounds."

"Oh yeah, definitely twins. Didn't they tell you when you heard the heart beat?"

"No, there was only one heartbeat."

"Hang on, I'm having another contraction. BYRON, PLEASE!"

Byron got closer to Ruby and started rubbing her neck and shoulders. He figured since she couldn't feel her legs maybe that would help her a little.

"Sometimes with twins the heart beat can be on the same beat and you will only think you are hearing one beat."

With that news Ruby actually passed out. Byron looked down at her and noticed that her hand went limp.

"Oh, god, help. Doc do something."

"If it is twins a C-section is her best bet. Especially since she has such a small frame."

The doctor left the room and a few minutes later came back with a hand held sonogram machine, he rubbed it over her large belly and sure enough on the little screen there were two little bundles in her oven. He showed Byron and he thought he was going to pass out.

"Then what are you waiting for let's go. I give you permission. I am her husband. Just make her be okay."

The doctor walked out of the room and told the nurses to go in and prep her for surgery. When the nurse hooked her up to a urine bag she woke up.

"I don't know what that was, but I know it hurt going in."

"Love, please, don't pass out on me like that again. My heart can't take it."

"I'm sorry. I'll try not to. Please tell me, what's going on right now, what did I miss?"

"The doctor says since it's twins, he wants to do a C-section on you. He says it will be the best way because you are so small. They're prepping you right now."

"Will you be able to go back there with me?"

"If you want me to, then I'll find a way."

"You know I want you to be there with me."

"I know what you want, I just like hearing you say it."

"They really do need to hurry up, I think our babies are pinching a nerve in my back and that is why I can't feel my legs."

"Roll over a little and I'll see what I can do."

"I don't think I can. I feel like a beached whale. I hurt and I want them out, now."

Dr. Toroya busted into the room and said, "Ruby, you better be nice to them."

"Dr. Toroya, I can't fell my legs, and I am fixing to have a C-section and why is it taking so long?"

"Well there maybe a person or two ahead of you. Hang on I'll see who I can bump down on the list."

Byron faced Ruby again and began stroking her cheek as Dr. Toroya disappeared out into the sterile hallway. Dr. Toroya bumped into the other doctor and they realized that Ruby was next in line for the OR. They both decided to go and give her the good news.

"Ruby in a few minutes we are going to wheel you down to surgery and you will meet your little babies. How do you feel?"

"I still can't feel my legs."

"I promise you, as soon as we get the babies out, the feeling in your legs will come back to you."

Just as promised, a few minutes later, Byron and the two doctors were wheeling her down to surgery. They had to make one hold up before going under the knife. The anesthesiologist wanted to dull her pain. He gave her a local spinal block. As soon as it went into her system she couldn't feel anything except for her face and hands. The doctors and nurses had her sprawled out on the table in the shape of a cross. Byron was at her head kissing her forehead and holding her hands. The doctors were on the other side of a blue sheet working on her. Dr. Toroya peeked over the sheet and said, "Hey, Ruby, can you feel this?"

"No, should I be able to?"

"No, I was just making sure the spinal was working right."

Byron said, "Thank you, Doc."

"Byron, if you want to see your children being born, you can stand up and look over the sheet."

"Thanks Doc, but I don't even like seeing Ruby cry, I think if I saw her being gutted like a fish I would probably pass out, and then I wouldn't be of any use to her right now."

"I'm glad you see it that way. But when I get them out I am going to hold them up in front of the sheet so you can see them."

"That's fine."

After a few minutes of silence from the doctors and a good bit of tugging Ruby heard Dr. Toroya say, "Baby A is out, and it's a boy."

Dr. Toroya held the baby up in front of Ruby and Bryon and then pulled him away so that he could get cleaned up. Byron had tears in his eyes when he looked at Ruby and said, "You gave me a son. I will always love you for that."

"Baby B is out, and it's a girl."

Again, Dr. Toroya held the baby up in front of Ruby and Byron and then he pulled her away so she could get cleaned up like her brother.

Ruby was so happy that she was crying. Byron was kissing her all over her face and hand he was holding. The doctors were sewing her up and stapling her stomach closed, then the nurses brought the babies back in to see her. Byron was so happy. You couldn't help but feel how excited he was. Ruby kissed both of the babies on the foreheads and Byron kissed them too. He was really gentle.

Then Dr. Toroya said, "Byron we are going to take Ruby down to recovery she will be there for one hour and then we will bring her back up to her room. If you want to go to you can, or you can go into the nursery with the babies."

"I'll go with Ruby; I want to see the babies when she does."

"Are you sure babe, you can go, its okay."

"No, don't you remember, I told you I would make sure you were okay first, I meant that."

"Dr. Toroya, there is no changing his mind once it's made up. Let's go."

Dr. Toroya and Byron were pushing her bed down to recovery where she was supposed to wait for a whole hour without her new babies. She thought Byron would have gone to see them. She was sincerely glad he didn't. She was still scared, she hadn't gotten the feeling back in her legs yet and that scared her more than anything else. When Dr. Toroya had her bed locked into position he walked out and said, "One hour guys."

"Ruby, if you slide over a little bit, I will lie beside you."

"I can't move. I'm numb all over. You can pull me slightly to the side and work your way in as long as you don't bump my stomach."

"I think I can manage that. Have you even noticed your stomach. You don't even look like you were pregnant."

"I think that is the nicest thing I have heard about my body in a while."

Byron walked over to the other side of the bed and pulled on the sheets to scoot her over, just a hair. He walked back to the other side and eased himself into the bed beside her. He watched her closely as she rubbed her hand over stomach and started crying again.

"Byron, they were just in there. This is weird. I don't think my body will be able to believe it until I see the babies again."

"You will see them, really soon. Now, lay back and let me worry about you. How do you feel?"

"I'm fine, the spinal is still working, and as a matter of fact I am feeling a little sleepy."

"Well, love, that is because it is five am. You are entitled to being a little sleepy after having major surgery and bringing twins into the world. Oh god, I should call the family."

"Actually, just call Cindy, I already gave her all the numbers. She knows who to call."

"That was sneaky, when did you do that?"

"When you and the contractors were outside working on the grounds for the shop."

"Well, I'm glad you did that. Now, I don't have a reason to move. I want to hold you. I am so proud of you Ruby. You have made me so happy. I have you, our son, and our daughter. Life really doesn't get any better than this. Although I do wish there was a way to go about getting them out, that didn't involve you being in pain."

"Byron, I'm . . . . fine."

Byron was still looking at Ruby and her eyes were drifting closed. He really was a proud papa. He got his whole family in one delivery. Ruby started snoring lightly and he wanted to comfort her so badly, he started running his fingers through her hair. Then he saw something that made him even happier. She twitched her legs. She wasn't immobile anymore. Thank God, he thought to himself. The hour in recovery seemed to take forever, but he was happy to lie beside his wife and watch her sleep.

Dr. Toroya came in the room and noticed Byron in bed with Ruby and she was sleeping. He knew Byron was in love with Ruby, because those beds were in no way comfortable, and to lay on one for an hour meant back pain later.

"Byron, how is she doing?"

"Well, she fell asleep about forty-five minutes ago, and she started twitching her legs a little."

"That's good. That means she was right, the babies were pinching a nerve. I am ready to roll her up to her room to see the babies."

With that being said Byron hopped out of the bed, carefully, he didn't want to wake Ruby. He helped Dr. Toroya push her back to her room. When they got to the room Byron saw Cindy and some of both of the families waiting with balloons and flowers. He was so happy that everyone wanted to share this time with them and come to see Ruby and the babies. Rubies mom was the first to step up and hug Byron. Once she started it the flood gates opened. Everyone had to come and hug him. He asked everyone to keep it down. He went into detail telling everyone what happened when they got to the hospital. Then he said, "Everyone Ruby gave birth to twins." Almost everyone in the room started crying. Not two seconds later, the nurses from earlier were wheeling in two bassinets. In the first was a small baby wrapped in a blue blanket. In the second was another small baby wrapped in a pink blanket.

"Everyone, I would like you to meet Mitchell Holden and Hailey Lynn Miller."

Ruby's mom and Cindy were crying and hugging each other. They kept asking each other if they knew she was having twins. Byron cut into that conversation. "No one knew we were having twins. Not even us. It was a surprise all around."

Just then Hailey lost her pacifier and she started crying. Ruby sat straight up searching for the sound. Byron leaned down to the bassinet and picked up his daughter and held her close to his heart. When Ruby saw how gentle he was being with the baby, she eased herself back onto the bed. She realized she probably shouldn't have moved that quickly. She felt a pinch in her stomach.

"Byron could you get Dr. Toroya, I think I might have pulled a staple loose."

Byron lifted her gown to see bandages that were tinged red from blood. He handed Hailey to Cindy and ran out of the room to search for the doctor. He was back in record time with Dr. Toroya right behind him. Dr. Toroya asked everyone to leave so he could check Ruby's bandages. Byron and the babies stayed right there. Dr. Toroya lifted her gown up, and pulled back the bandages. There was blood, but it was from the surgery. She was fine. No bleeding and no pulled staples.

"Ruby, please, don't sit up like that again, okay. I'm not a cardiologist and if Byron has a heart attack I won't know exactly what to do."

"I'm sorry, when I heard the baby cry I thought something was wrong. Then I felt that pinch, all I could think was that I ripped one of the staples out."

Byron said, "I'm glad you were concerned for the babies, but please, let me take care of them and you until you are able to move around."

"Byron that's a great idea. Ruby, you should listen to your husband. He knows what he's talking about. You will be here for the next four days, so for those four days you have no choice, but to take it easy. Tomorrow you can get out of bed and go to the bathroom on your own again."

"Thank you Dr. Toroya, I really am sorry. I didn't mean to scare either of you."

"That's okay, now get some rest, you have two babies to take home with you when you go and that can mean some restless nights."

Dr. Toroya turned to the doorway and left Ruby's room. Byron walked closer to Ruby and pulled her gown back down right as her family was walking in the door.

"Byron could you help me. The remote to the bed is over my head could you push the button that helps me sit up. I want to talk to everyone. I want to hold our babies."

Ruby gave Byron the sweetest smile and he couldn't help himself he leaned down in front of family and friends and kissed his wife. Then he got right in her ear and said, "Thank you, love. For all of this."

Byron handed Hailey to Ruby first. She was so excited. She got exactly what she had wanted from the beginning. She got her girl, that she planned on dressing up all the time and Byron got his boy, someone he could teach sports to and do guy stuff with. She kissed her new daughter on the forehead and passed her to her mom. Slowly Hailey made it in a full circle. Everyone wanted to hold the two bundles. Byron then placed Mitchell in Ruby's awaiting arms. He was a little heavier than his sister, but that was fine. Maybe that meant he would take after his daddy. She kissed his forehead and also passed him around to her mom. When both the babies made it around the room, Byron laid them back in the bassinets and pulled the blanket down off of their heads. Ruby started crying. Hailey had auburn hair, just like the girl from her dreams. Mitchell had darker hair and it was thick. She was surprised at how much Byron's son really looked like him, when he got older there would be no telling them apart, she thought to herself.

Byron was watching Ruby stare at the babies and when he saw her tear up he choked up a little, too. His life was complete and he knew it. He didn't need anything else to make him happy. He had it all.

It was about nine o'clock in the morning when everyone left the hospital. Byron asked them if they would mind coming back later. He and Ruby needed to rest. Byron called the nursery and two nurses came into their room and wheeled the babies down the hall to where they could look after them until Byron and Ruby woke up again. When the babies were gone, Byron helped Ruby slide over in her bed and he laid himself beside her again. He kissed her gently on the lips, then the kiss turned a little more intimate. He fought his urges. He could kiss her now, but he would be waiting for a while to make love to her. He wasn't sure he could wait the four weeks the doctor spoke of, but if it would help Ruby, then he was going to try. Ruby broke the kiss off and leaned slightly toward Byron and rested her hand on his chest. They laid there in complete silence thinking about how their lives had just completely changed for the better. Byron was the first to fall asleep this time and Ruby watched him dream as his eyes danced behind his eye lids. She didn't feel tired as of right now. She just wanted to be with her man. In any way that she could. She loved the fact that he didn't want to sleep on the little sleeper sofa. Of course, he was too long for it anyway, but still she told herself he just wanted to snuggle up to her. She started humming in her sleep and soon she was under.

*   *   *

"Byron, I have to pee. Wake up. Can you go and get the nurse? Dr. Toroya said I could get up today, and I really need to get out of this bed."

Byron sat up slowly and stretched then said, "Yeah, hang on a second. I'll be right back."

Byron got out of bed and started off to the nurse's station and started asking for Dr. Toroya.

"Is she okay?" One of the nurses asked.

"Yeah, she said she wants to go pee, and Dr. Toroya said she could get up today."

"Okay, I will be right there."

Byron made his way back to their room and noticed Ruby had her legs crossed.

"Byron is he coming I really have to pee and I don't like how it burns with this stupid catheter."

"A nurse is coming, she will be here in just a second."

Ruby kept her legs crossed and closed her eyes. She was trying to put it out of her mind.

A nurse came in the room and said, "Ruby, if you'll spread your legs just a little, I can get that tube out of there."

"Ruby willingly spread her legs, then slid down on the bed. She reached out for Byron's hand and he grabbed her. She held on tight. That tube burned more coming out than it did going in. Once the nurse had everything that was constricting her removed, she told Ruby to try to move over so she could swing her legs over the side of the bed. Ruby looked up into Byron's face and said, "If I fall . . ."

"You won't fall. I won't let you."

The nurse took a step back to let Byron help her. Ruby got her feet over the edge of the bed and they were hanging freely. The nurse told her to wait there and let the blood move around in her veins. Ruby sat there and held Byron's hand tight. When she felt like she was going to wet herself she used him to pull herself upright. She was standing, and taking baby steps to the bathroom. Byron reached around behind him and opened the door. He helped Ruby get to the toilet and Ruby said, "Babe, you don't have to wait with me. I know you don't want to see this."

"Have you lost your mind. I'm not leaving you alone, now. It's just blood Ruby."

"I'm glad you have the stomach to see it that way."

Ruby asked Byron to pull the door shut, and she let the gown drop to the floor. It had never been tied and it was becoming a bother trying to keep it closed. She was with her husband, she didn't care if he saw her naked, even though she didn't feel especially pretty right now. She reached to try and pull down those boy shorts they gave everyone who had a baby, they were made of material similar to an ace bandage, and one size fit all. She couldn't get them free. Byron put her hands around his neck and he reached down and lowered them for her. She grabbed his arm with one hand while she removed the pad that contained the bloody evidence of her after birth. Gross, she thought to herself. She threw the pad into the biohazard trash can and Byron helped her to sit down on the toilet. She peed a river. She felt so relieved to have all that liquid out of her system. When she finished, she reached a hand out and Byron was there. She grabbed his hand and pulled herself upright again. He had already put a pad in the boy shorts and he knelt down in front of her. She put her hands on his shoulders to steady herself as he lifted one foot then the other, he pulled the makeshift underwear into place and since he was still on his knees he could see the bandages. He pulled the tape back and took a peek. She looked like she had train tracks running across her bikini line. He put the bandage back into place and helped her to the sink. She really wanted to brush her teeth and wash her face. She felt really gross. She didn't want to kiss Byron while she looked and smelled like this, but she knew he wouldn't have made a big deal out of it, anyway.

When she was all clean and smelling a little bit better she reached her hands up and wrapped them around his neck, then he leaned down a little and she kissed him feather light but continuous kisses. She felt disgusting right now, like the bride of Frankenstein. She also needed to feel loved, and when Byron would kiss her that was usually all it took. He ended the kiss and said, "Ruby, there will plenty of time for that when I get you in that bed, come on let's get you off of your feet. Do you want to sit in the rocking chair?"

"Yeah I think I would like that better than the bed."

She started walking out of the bathroom and the nurse was still there. She said they were in there a while and she wanted to make sure everything was okay.

Byron told her everything was fine, then asked if she could call the nursery and have them bring up the Miller twins. The nurse told him it was no problem. Byron helped Ruby into the rocking chair then stuffed a few pillows in around her. She looked so fragile. When the babies came into the room her mood changed completely. She became this doting mom. "Byron I want to hold both of them."

"At the same time?"

"Yeah, I can handle it. I did it for nine months, a few minutes isn't going to kill me."

"Alright love, what ever you want."

Byron picked up Mitchell and laid him in her right arm since that was her strongest arm, then he picked up Hailey and laid her down in Ruby's left arm. Byron took a step back and watched Ruby rock them and kiss them so tenderly. He knew he was home, and he had his family.

While holding her new little bundles of joy she looked up and saw Byron staring at her. She had to ask. She just couldn't help herself.

"Byron, what are you thinking about right now?"

"I'm thinking that I love you, and I love our babies. I love you because you went through that pain to give me these babies. That really means a lot."

"Well love, that's what I'm here for. I love you, too. More than you know. Now tell me, do I look like a mom? Because you definitely look like a happy daddy."

"You are the most beautiful mother anyone in this hospital has ever seen, and the most resilient I think."

Byron kissed her softly again and then sat there beside her rocking chair and they enjoyed this sweet moment with their new family.

THE END